THE KILLER INSIDE THEM

A. S. FRENCH

NEONOIR BOOKS

ALSO BY A. S. FRENCH

Crime Fiction and Thrillers

The Astrid Snow series

Book one: Don't Fear the Reaper.

Book two: The Killing Moon.

Book three: Lost in America.

Book four: Gone to Texas

The Detective Jen Flowers series

Book one: The Hashtag Killer.

Book two: Serial Killer.

Book three: Night Killer.

Book four: The Killer Inside Them

Northern Crime Fiction

Where The Bodies Are Buried

Crime Short Stories

Call Me: An Astrid Snow Short Story

Dark Snow: An Astrid Snow Short Story

Writing as Andrew. S. French

Science Fiction

The Time Traveller's Murder

The Arcane Supernatural Thriller Series

Book one: The Arcane.

Book two: The Arcane Identity.

The Ella Finn Fantasy Novella Series

Ella and the Elementals

Ella and the Multiverse

Ella and the Monsters

Ella and the Dreamers

Supernatural Short Stories

Dead Souls.

Go to www.andrewsfrench.com for more information.

1 PANDORA: THE RESCUE

I knew before the weekend was over, I'd kill someone.

However, today was different. I saved a life. It was ten years too late, but it happened.

Exhaust fumes filled the air and my lungs as the pensioner stood frozen in the middle of the road. A flock of seagulls squawked above him as I gripped the lamppost, the metal chilling my skin. There were others around me, London's Saturday morning shoppers and tourists, but they only stared at him.

The old man resembled a tree in a petrified forest. A wrinkled face peered out from under the brim of a black hat, his eyes heavily lidded and weighed down by the dark lines covering his skin. He was stooped over, shopping bags in both hands as if he was a living sculpture by Anthony Gormley.

It wasn't the sea heading straight for him, but a motorbike going at full tilt, one of those that delivered barely edible food which was cold before you got it. But not as cold as the old man. His skin chilled my hand as I leapt into the middle of the road and dragged him away. The tyres screamed as the bike missed me by inches, or so I thought until I sat both of us down. Just below my knee, the trouser was torn and dark red. I touched it and my fingers came away wet. Something unpleasant surged up that leg, but I ignored it and phoned for an ambulance. I couldn't tell if he was in shock or suffering a heart attack, but his eyes were glazed over and he was unmoving.

One of the bags tumbled over, spilling fresh fruit and rotten vegetables over the pavement. The smell of decomposing carrots assaulted my nose while people strolled by without a care in the world. I glanced up to see the take-away driver stuck at a red light, his helmeted head aimed at us as he waved his fist. If my leg hadn't felt like it was in a microwave, I might have chased after him.

'Are you okay?' The old man didn't respond. 'Can you hear me?'

I took his hand in mine, checking to see if there was a pulse. It was there, but very faint. There was a scar on his cheek that looked as if he'd tried to shave that day and the blade had refused to cut through the leather of his skin. I gazed into his pale blue eyes, seeing an echo of my father there, of how he was before the memories went and he forgot to feed himself.

As we waited for the ambulance, he told me his name was Tommy. We spent the time getting to know each other, though I did all the talking. I continued to grip his hand, hoping some human contact and the sound of my voice would keep him stable and bring him out of his inertia.

'I'm Pandora and I grew up around here.'

I glanced at our surroundings, staring at all the things I didn't recognise, all the new buildings and shops which had sprung up while I was away. I was the only person with my head held high; everyone else was bent over, gazing into digital devices and oblivious to the world. Headphones dangled from their ears; they preferred listening to electronic voices rather than actual ones, choosing recorded sounds over what was in the air. Still, you either forget everything or remember everything with the right music.

I didn't blame them. There is comfort in finding connections through technology, especially if you don't have any in the real world. I was thinking about what I'd lost when the old man squeezed my hand. His lips trembled as he spoke, only moving on one side of his face.

'What happened?'

'You had an accident. The ambulance will take you to the hospital.' It had pulled up next to us, its flashing lights hurting my eyes. He gripped my fingers again, finding a strength I'd thought beyond him a second ago.

'You won't leave me, will you?'

Daggers stabbed at my heart when I recognised the fear in his face.

'Where are your family and friends?'

A sheen of grey clouded his eyes. 'I don't have anyone. They're all gone.'

Many things separated us. Gender, upbringing, circumstance and at least forty years of experience, but we shared that one thing. We were solitary humans, not by choice, but by chance. He lifted a trembling arm and put it around me as the paramedics approached. One guided him to the ambulance while the other spoke to me.

'Are you a relative?' What could I say? Not by blood, but something else had bonded us. 'If you are, you can go with him.' He noticed my wound before I could reply. 'What happened here?'

'A motorbike clipped me when I dragged the old man from the road.'

'You better come with us anyway.'

I didn't argue. It was the first bit of company I'd had in a week.

My knee creaked as I climbed into the back of the ambulance. The paramedics strapped the pensioner into a seat and checked him over. They asked him questions, which he mumbled answers to while he peered at me. His lips shook as he mouthed those words again.

Please don't leave me.

'I won't,' I said, knowing it was a lie.

He'd closed his eyes by the time we got to the hospital. Even so, he reached out a trembling hand to me. I took it as the paramedics led us inside the building.

'Help me,' he whispered as they wheeled him into a ward.

But how could I help him when I couldn't help myself?

2 JEN: THE GAME

The screaming wounded my brain. I'm sure it had nothing to do with my hangover.

The screams increased, so loud they drowned out the thump of the rain bouncing off my head, the air so cold it hurt my teeth. The weather forecast was a brisk but sunny day, but I should have known better for early September in England. I also should have worn a raincoat or brought my brolly. Only I didn't own an umbrella, and I wanted to show off my new jacket.

God knows why, though. I dragged my head up from staring at the ground and the soup of mud washing over my shoes. The air stank of dead meat drifting off an unseen burger van. The shouting grew more boisterous, coming from a horde of men and women here to watch their little darlings hoofing a football in the downpour.

I appeared to be the only one aware of the horrendous conditions, guessing it was because the rest of them were more invested in their children's sporting endeavours. The rain seeped into my face as I wiped it from my eyes, searching for Abbey on the pitch closest to me – six games were going on simultaneously – struggling to find her in a sea of teenage legs and excitement.

She'd surprised me several times over the last two years, but I thought she was joking when she said she'd joined the girls' school football team. I realised she was serious when she spent her pocket money on a pair of football boots, but I assumed she was going through her usual short-term obsession with one thing before moving on to another. Music had been that fixation now for six months and she took it seriously, writing songs with her best friend Francine and practising with their band three nights a week. I didn't mind about the mess they left everywhere or how their tunes had upset the cat so much, she'd started leaving little bundles of shit around the house. I even liked some of their music. Abbey appeared dedicated to it, recording stuff on the computer and uploading it to various websites. The online interactions made me nervous, but I understood it was part of the process. It wasn't affecting her schoolwork; it had sparked a new impetus in Abbey to do well in her subjects, so I was happy to let her continue her musical obsession.

Yet I was a little startled to think she might give all of that up for football, though also glad because I was worried about her getting involved in the music business full time as she grew older. But when she told me she was continuing with the band and playing for the team, my concern was different.

'How will you do all that, love, and keep up with your schoolwork?'

She brushed off the question with a wave of her hand.

'Oh, Mum, you worry if I don't have hobbies, and then you fret if I do.'

So here I was on a wet and windy Saturday morning, watching the game and trying to remember what I knew about football, while all around me, the other adults were acting as if it was the World Cup Final.

A woman shouted so loudly next to me, I thought she was crawling into my ear. The rain increased, sweeping across my face as I stared at the harpy, her teeth promising to leap from her mouth as she bawled at the girls attempting to kick the ball through the mud. Perhaps she was the team's manager, but it seemed more likely she was a parent. I glared at her through the downpour, but she ignored me.

I turned from her and focused on the pitch, searching for Abbey and finding her sliding towards me. I thought she was leaving the game for a second until she took the ball from an opponent and sprinted for the opposition goal. She skimmed past two players and thudded the ball into the top corner of the net; my mouth was so wide it was like a fleshly bucket catching the rain. I spat into the grass and shouted with the rest of the crowd, all apart from the noisy woman next to me who had a face borrowed from a cadaver. I guessed she was supporting the other team.

'Abbey's the best player here by a country mile.'

I turned to my side to see Francine, my daughter's best friend and the other half in the two girl musical combo Abbey fronted. She was dressed tip to toe in black, a singular dark presence in this terrible weather. There was more makeup on her face than usual, a sludge of Stygian charcoal so thick, even the rain couldn't make a dent in it. A hood covered her head, I guessed not just to hold off the downpour, but because she was embarrassed by her alopecia.

'I thought you were on the team, Francine.'

Earlier in the year, she'd wanted to be called Ladybird, but she seemed to have forgotten about the name change.

She pulled her top closer to her eyes, obscuring the one closest to me as if wanting to hide her face.

'Something came up at home, Ms Flowers, so I had to miss this game.' She glanced at the team, watching them control the ball in difficult conditions. 'It looks like they're doing okay without me.'

'What position do you play?' I knew Abbey was a striker because she'd spent all the car ride telling me.

'I'm the number ten who plays off Abbey, like Lionel Messi.'

I nodded, vaguely knowing who that was. The shouty woman had inched towards me, listening to our conversation. I stared into her agitated eyes.

'Can I help you?'

She pointed at Abbey on the pitch. 'Is she yours?'

Her voice shook as she made it sound like I'd purchased Abbey from a slave market.

'She's my daughter, if that's what you mean?'

'How old is she?' Her hand trembled as if strangling an invisible rabbit. 'She looks about eighteen, and these kids are all supposed to be under sixteen.'

Abbey was fifteen, but I could see what the woman meant. Looking at my daughter as she defied the conditions and glided across the muddy pitch like a gazelle, I realised she'd grown a lot in the last few months, gaining a few inches in height and confidence in her manner, so she appeared more of a young woman than a girl.

'She's under sixteen.' As I spoke, Abbey scored another goal. 'I guess she's just better than the other girls.'

I tried not to smile, but couldn't help myself. The woman swore under her breath and turned from me.

'Are you upsetting people again, Jen?'

A familiar voice spoke at my side. I kept my gaze on the game as I replied.

'I didn't know you liked school football, Detective Inspector Monroe.'

My partner touched my shoulder, his fingers protected by a stylish glove.

'I go where the wind takes me.'

I turned to face him. 'I'm surprised you're not halfway down the Thames in this weather.'

He removed his hand and shook the water from the leather. 'Abbey told me she was playing today and I promised I wouldn't miss it.' He stared at the game. 'It seems like she's the star player as well.'

I nodded as the rain stopped and the halftime whistle went.

'Is there somewhere to get something warm to eat and drink?'

'Of course. I know the best pie and Bovril place in London, and it's five minutes from here. Shall we go?'

I didn't need asking twice. Jack led me away as I left Francine to join her teammates as they dried out in one of the changing rooms. We trudged through the mud towards a mobile food van and joined the small queue. Two minutes later, we were served and I was warming my hands on a hot drink. As I did so, a commotion centred around a group of six people striding into the field.

I nodded at the hubbub. 'Do you think they're gangsters?'

He laughed in between slurping at his Bovril.

'Don't you know who that is?'

I shook my head. 'Should I?'

'Then I'll enlighten you, DI Flowers. The tall bloke in his fifties with the lean, chiselled cheeks, dimpled chin, steel-blue eyes, distinguished grey hair and permanent smile is Robert Randolph.'

I stared across at the man, watching as he signed autographs for a bunch of over-excited adults.

'I still don't know who he is.'

Jack finished his coffee and dropped the empty cup into a bin.

'He formed a tech company twenty years ago, and now he's a multi-millionaire.'

'Who's the woman with him?' She seemed a lot younger than Randolph and looked like she'd just come from a shopping trip at Harrods.

'That's his wife, Grace.'

I sipped at my drink. 'Why do you think they're here?'

The rain had disappeared, but it was still freezing.

'Who knows what goes through the minds of the rich, Jen? Perhaps they want to buy the land and build houses on it.'

With the heat returning to my frozen bits, we returned to the game. As we did, a young woman dressed all in pink and wearing the tallest of high-heels approached us. She smiled at Jack, and I assumed it was his niece until I remembered he was an only child. The walking salmon threw her arms around his neck, and his face turned the same colour as her clothes as she kissed him. My jaw dropped as a few of the soccer moms whispered amongst themselves. The few blokes there gazed at my partner through green eyes.

After thirty seconds that seemed like an eternity, the woman, perhaps twenty years old, pulled away from Jack. He puffed out his rosy cheeks and stumbled over his words.

'Jen, this is Tiffany.'

I didn't know what to say as Tiffany stuck out ring-covered fingers towards me.

'Jack has told me so much about you.'

I grasped the younger woman's hand, noticing how perfect her skin was, and realised she smelt of peaches.

'He's told me nothing about you, Tiffany.'

She squeezed my fingers and laughed. 'Call me Tiff.' She glanced at Jack. 'I think he's trying to keep me a secret.'

'Well, it worked.' I arched my eyebrows at him. 'How do you two know each other?'

Tiffany replied for him. 'We met online a month ago.' She threaded her arm into his as the players readied for the second half. 'He's such a sweetie for an old bloke.'

Before Jack could respond, the referee blew her whistle and Tiffany released her beau. She turned to a group of women behind us and marched towards them in those impossible heels. They were all the same age as her, decked out in clothes so brightly coloured, you could have hung them from the end of a rainbow.

I shook my head at him when she was out of earshot.

'How old is she?'

The pink returned to his cheeks.

'She'll be twenty-one next year.'

I whistled long and loud. 'Jesus, Jack. You're nearly twice her age.' I knew he'd struggled since his wife had thrown him out, but this was a bit much.

'Age is no barrier to happiness, partner.'

'Have you been reading fortune cookies again?'

He grinned as the players kicked off. 'Don't you want me to be happy, Jen?'

I kept my eye on Abbey as I replied.

'I don't want you to make a fool of yourself.' I glanced at Tiffany giggling with her friends. 'And I'd rather you didn't have a heart attack.'

He laughed so hard, I thought he might have a cardiac arrest there and then.

'Don't worry about me, partner; I'll be fine. It's you I'm concerned about.'

Abbey waved at me as she ran through the mud.

'Concerned about what?'

'You know what. Have you told Abbey yet?'

I dragged him to the side. 'What happened is between you and me. And you promised to keep it to yourself.'

He stared at me as if I was on the verge of a nervous breakdown, and perhaps I was. The secret I was keeping from my daughter was that I thought I'd heard a message on our answering machine from my estranged father a few months back. I'd only told Jack about it one drunken night when I couldn't keep it to myself anymore.

'Of course I will, Jen. I was just, well, wondering if it had happened again.'

A volcano erupted inside my veins.

'You want to know if I imagined my father calling me again.' I glared at him. 'No, Jack, that hasn't happened.'

Not yet, anyway. The idea I might lose my mind was never far from my thoughts.

'It was stress-related, Jen. Which isn't a surprise considering what you were going through.'

That's what he believed and what I'd told myself many times since. But it wasn't the complete story. There was something in my past I'd never revealed to anyone, not even him, which weighed on my mind and needed to be confronted. But not now. This was Abbey's morning and I wouldn't let anything ruin that. As I turned to the pitch, she scored her third goal; a perfect opportunity to change the subject.

'Don't they call that a hat-trick?'

'They do. She must have inherited all of her talents from you, partner.'

His words swirled inside my head as I watched Abbey celebrating with her teammates, my brain thinking about what else she may have got from me.

3 PANDORA: THE HOSPITAL

The place smelt of antiseptic and cleaning fluids. I ran my fingers over my leg, watching them come away red and damp as I peered around my environment.

I find hospitals unnerving. For most of us, they're the places where we start and end our lives. And in between those points, trips to the hospital indicate illness or poor health, or visits to people suffering from one or the other. So no matter how marvellous the NHS staff is, I still try to avoid them at all costs. As a child, I'd had an emergency tonsillectomy, where the doctor performed the procedure with a penknife on my local GP surgery floor. So I owe my life to NHS personnel's dedication and quick-wittedness.

Yet here I was in Accident and Emergency waiting for a medical professional to look at my leg. As soon as the ambulance arrived at A and E, the medics wheeled Tommy off to see a nurse. He didn't appear too shaken up by the incident, but the staff thought he might have had a stroke. I'm no doctor, but from the way he stood transfixed in the road, I realised something serious must have happened to him. Our brief conversation on the way to hospital also told me he was lonely.

The nurse found a bus pass in his wallet plus an address, but no phone number. He had no mobile or contact number for family or friends. I assumed the medics hoped I was his daughter, but I had to disappoint them. I hadn't been a daughter for a long time.

The ache in my leg returned as the sick and the injured kept on coming. It was a good job it was a Saturday afternoon and not the night; otherwise, the place would have been full of drunks and those itching for a scrap. Still, when I glanced around the room, a few people were exhibiting signs of pharmaceutical ingestion.

A bloke next to me was staring at his phone, watching a politician give a news conference. My companion had a face stolen from a Dali painting, with eyes plucked from the bowels of hell. The bags under his eyes gripped his nose as he pointed at the screen and ranted at me.

'This is why we're stuck for hours in here, because of bastards like him, the lying toe rag.' I didn't disagree, but tried not to give him any encouragement. But he didn't need it. 'You've never reached the end of the line with him. He's the shit that sticks to the bottom of your shoe, that bedraggled thing that crawls out of the sewer to nuzzle up to you, the turd that won't flush, the show that's still on the screens decades after it became boring. He's that fat garden weed you can never get rid of no matter how much poison you dump on it; he's that awful creature which clings to the wall in a horror movie.'

As a hospital security guard inched his way towards us, I nodded in silence. That was the last thing I needed: someone to come over and start asking questions, maybe going through my bag and seeing the illegal things I kept there.

The ranting man realised impending doom was on him if he didn't shut up, so he did. After his rant, I'd expected to be stuck there for hours, but I only had to wait thirty minutes before someone came and patched me up. The bike had done more damage to my trousers than my leg, but my flesh didn't think so.

I was heading out when a nurse called me over.

'Tommy would like to see you.'

'Do you know what happened to him?'

'A mild stroke. I'm told he was in the middle of the road when it struck, and you risked your life to save him.'

'Anyone would have done the same.' Or perhaps my subconscious forced me to save a life before taking one, a universal balance guided by an unseen hand. 'What happens to him now?'

'We'll keep him in for a few days, see how he gets on. But it seems like he lives on his own and has no family.'

'What about social services? Won't they organise help for him?'

'If they need to, yes.' She peered straight into my eyes. 'Perhaps you might visit him while he's here.'

I had a lot to do in the next few days, but I didn't tell her what, for how could I explain to a stranger I had people to kill and saving someone had only been an accident? I kept that information for my diary.

'I'll see what I can do.'

She smiled and took me to the ward. Tommy was sitting in bed peering at a TV on the wall opposite, staring at a group of men dressed like chickens as they tried to climb across a rope ladder. I assumed it was a game show and not the latest induction of new Members of Parliament. I cleared my throat to get his attention. As he turned to me, I couldn't help but think of a waxwork I witnessed in Madame Tussauds many years ago of an actor playing a zombie.

'I don't need any coal, love, but thanks anyway.'

I sat in the chair nearest him, noticing that both sides of his face were working now.

'I'm not delivering coal, Tommy. I'm the one who pulled you out of the road. Did the nurses tell you about that?'

His eyes lit up like lightbulbs as he stretched out two wrinkled, trembling hands towards me.

'Oh, they did.' His grip was reminiscent of touching a turtle. 'I can't thank you enough, love. You're an angel come down to Earth, you are.'

I smiled at him. 'Do you have any relatives who can look after you, Tommy?'

He let go of me and sat back on the bed. Three women in bikinis that barely covered their bits were squirming inside baths of beans on the TV screen.

'I had a daughter once, but I lost her.' Thick shadows consumed his face. 'It's only me now.' A glaze descended across his eyes. 'But I've always got you, haven't I, Emma.'

I was wondering what to say when a nurse entered the room.

'Emma was his daughter.' She handed him a glass of water and two pills. 'It's time for your painkillers, Tommy.'

'What do you mean was?' I said when she'd finished with him.

'She passed away three years ago.' She moved closer to me so as not to upset him with the news. 'It was a hit-and-run driver who was never caught. Tommy was living with her, but he's been on his own ever since.' She removed the glass from his hands. 'Though I'm not sure how he ended up in the middle of the road. He should have a social worker monitoring him and carers visiting him every day.'

I didn't argue with her, instead looking at him as he gazed at the nonsense on the TV. I turned to leave, reaching the door as he spoke to me.

'Bring me some fags tomorrow, will you, Emma? I haven't had a smoke in a long time.'

I left him dreaming of cigarettes as a notification pinged on my phone. It was in my hand as I strode into the corridor, noticing the commotion in reception and the arrival of the security guards to sort it out. I assumed the ranting man had gone ballistic again.

I checked the message confirming my date for tonight.

A date. How exciting.

And I hadn't had a date in a long time.

There would be no going back after it.

And even Tommy wouldn't want to know me then.

4 JEN: THE HOSPITAL

The game ended 8-0, with Abbey grabbing five goals. The weather now matched the mood of her celebrating team, all warmth and smiles, though the air still smelt of wet grass. The sun kissed my face as she finished hugging her teammates and ran to me.

'What did you think, Mum?' Her grin was big enough to swallow the sky.

'You were fantastic, Abs.'

'She's an England star in the making, Mrs Flowers.'

The woman speaking was the manager, Beth Rigsby, who I'd met before the match. She'd made the same mistake then about my name, but I couldn't be bothered correcting her. Every time I looked at her, I imagined her wearing a shabby cardigan and kicking a cat.

'I thought the whole team played well, Beth.'

She placed an unwanted arm on my shoulder and pulled me from the girls.

'Indeed, but between you and me, I think the scouts will be out to watch Abbey sooner rather than later.'

I wriggled free from her grasp. 'Scouts?'

An unfortunate image of John Wayne scooping up my daughter and riding away bounced through my head.

'From the big teams in the Women's Premier League.' She got close enough I couldn't ignore the lemon hairspray keeping her barnet in one piece. 'I know someone at Chelsea and can put in a good word for Abbey.'

'Wasn't today only the second game she's played?'

Her head moved up and down so fast, she resembled a manic nodding dog.

'Yes, yes, but she's been great in training the last two weeks, and word spreads quickly in the game nowadays. All the professional clubs are always looking for talent and trying to snatch up the best young prospects.'

'Well, let's see how she goes, shall we?' As I spoke, Abbey pulled on my arm.

'Mum, Coach Rigsby is taking the squad out for pizza to celebrate. Is it okay for me to go?'

'Of course, love.' I smiled at Rigsby. 'Just give me the name of the restaurant and I'll pick you up later.'

'I'll text you when I'm ready, Mum. Are you going home?'

'Probably.' It felt wrong to lie to her, but I didn't want Abbey to know where I was going.

I left them to it, watching Jack and his new girlfriend swooning in each other's arms as she led him towards the Randolphs and their entourage. By the time I reached the car, I was nearly dried out, but the dryness in my throat made it difficult to breathe. I had an appointment to keep, one I'd been avoiding for at least ten years.

The sound of Abbey's happiness still lingered in my head as my phone vibrated with a message. I fastened the seatbelt and checked the mobile, expecting something from

Jack, surprised to receive a text from the place I was getting ready to visit.

Your appointment at The Redwood Nursing Home has been cancelled because the resident has had a fall. An ambulance has taken her to St Luke's Hospital. We will be in touch to rearrange your appointment in the future.

The message's impersonal nature made me think it was a standard text for cancellations, but it didn't matter too much; St Luke's was only another five minutes away. So I started the car and drove off, preparing myself for a reunion with my mother.

———

AS I ENTERED and headed for the reception, the building crawled with people. I pushed my way to the front and showed a harassed woman behind the desk my warrant card. A sense of relief covered her face when she saw me.

'Oh, thank goodness you're here.' She pointed towards a group arguing with staff near the far wall. 'They refuse to behave themselves, swearing at everyone and threatening violence.'

I put my ID away. 'Where's hospital security?'

She shook her head. 'I don't know.' Her eyes scrutinised me. 'Are you sure you can handle them?' She bent closer to whisper to me. 'I think they're from a well-known crime family.'

'Did you call the police?'

Her face darkened. 'I believe someone did.'

As she replied, the oldest man in the group swore to kill one of the staff.

'That's not why I'm here. My mother was brought to the

hospital about twenty minutes ago after a fall in her nursing home.'

'Oh.' You could have dropped a fruit basket into her mouth. 'So you won't help us?'

The noise increased from that corner, most of it comprising incessant swearing. Before I could reply, the security arrived and defused the situation. The receptionist breathed a sigh of relief as I spoke to her.

'I'm here to see Ruth Flowers.'

She checked her computer, the narrowness of her eyes telling me she wasn't too happy regarding my lack of involvement in the public disturbance.

'She's on ward six, but visiting times are not for another hour.'

I peered right through her. 'Which way is it?'

She pointed behind me. 'It's on the first floor, but they won't let you in now.'

I smiled and went to the stairs, knowing nothing would stop me from seeing my mother. I'd put it off for a decade, and if I faltered again, I'd talk myself into avoiding her for the rest of my life. And I couldn't do that. There was one thing I needed to know from her, and I wouldn't leave the hospital until I got it; visiting hours or not.

It was a three-minute trek upstairs. I found myself at another desk, but with less commotion this time. Again, a staff member tried to tell me to go, but my ID card soon silenced them.

'I need to see my mother, Ruth Flowers.'

'Wait here.'

It was a stern two words, heavy with displeasure. So I did as instructed, casting my gaze around the ward, impressed as always by the NHS staff's hard work and dedi-cation. This wasn't the hospital where I'd had Abbey, but it was very similar, and the staff that day had made a difficult situation bearable. Still, as much as I loved my daughter, I knew I wouldn't be having any more. Fourteen hours in labour was enough to put any woman off sex.

Not that I'd had many opportunities recently. I was thinking of my last sexual dalliance when a handsome doctor strode towards me with the warmest of smiles.

'Mrs Flowers?'

'Ms.' A kaleidoscope of butterflies burst forth inside my stomach.

'If you'd like to follow me, I'll take you to your mother's room.' I stood at his side, the smell of the antiseptic in the air making me dizzy. 'Did the care home inform you of what happened?'

I searched for a name badge on his uniform, but there wasn't one. 'No, doctor, they didn't.' It didn't feel right to tell him I hadn't seen her in a decade, and I was only there for myself and not her. And maybe for Abbey.

He talked as he went, with me keeping up like a sidekick.

'As you're aware, your mother was diagnosed with dementia ten years ago, though, from a glance at the medical records from her GP, she probably had the early stages of it well before that.'

I grabbed his arm to stop him. 'Do you have any idea when?'

His furrowed brow didn't put me at ease. 'How old is your mother? Sixty?' I nodded. 'So, her official diagnosis was at fifty, but you may have noticed the first stages in her behaviour ten or fifteen years before that.' He removed a digital device from his pocket. 'How old were you when your mother was thirty-five?'

'Eleven,' I said.

He peered into his screen, which I guessed wasn't his mobile phone.

'Do you remember any instances which might have indicated she was having problems with her memory?'

'I'm not sure, doctor.'

The azure of his eyes made me feel as if I was about to sink into a Caribbean sea.

'In the first stage, people with dementia experience something is not right, perhaps claiming their memory is playing up. They might feel embarrassed or frightened when they recognise changes in their memory or thinking. Family and friends question and comment on the changes and forgetfulness. The person is likely to fight to keep up the façade of "normality" and being in control. They might do things, such as making up a little story to fill the memory gap of someone or something they can't remember. Professionals label this gap-filling as "confabulation". However, this storytelling or gap filling does not mean the person is telling a lie. It's actually a creative self-defence mechanism that helps the person keep up the façade.' The digital hue of the screen was reflected in his eyes. 'You'll have been too young to notice this, but any adults around you might have been aware.'

'I recall one time, doctor.' It returned to me after I'd heard his words. 'My mother couldn't find her glasses. So she asked me if I'd seen them.'

'What happened then?'

'I told her they were on her bedside table. She accused me of putting them there because she didn't.'

'That could have been an early indicator,' he said.

'My father worked full time, volunteering every night and weekend at the church. He joked that her forgetfulness was because she was a sinner and should come to church with him, but she refused. So he took me instead.'

I moved away from the doctor and pressed my back into the wall. He must have seen the anguish in my eyes, mistaking it for guilt.

'You couldn't have known what was wrong with your mother, Ms Flowers; you were too young to comprehend what was happening to her. In the second stage, people with dementia are far more relaxed and inclined to give in and let go. They withdraw and appear preoccupied with the past, thinking back to happy times, restoring old memories, and sometimes living in that time and reality. Their way of communicating changes too. Sentence construction may not be as clear. They might start a sentence making perfect sense, but then it becomes muddled in the middle and ends as something hard to understand. But sometimes, observers who aren't trained professionals look upon this type of behaviour as just forgetfulness or tiredness after a stressful day.'

I recognised his attempt to make me feel better, and I appreciated it. After the glasses incident, it had been two or three years later when she'd started getting names mixed up, confusing days of the week, or forgetting who my father's friends from church were. That's when I noticed how much she was drinking. That stuck with me, but her memory loss didn't unless I was connecting the two. Her memory was failing because she drank, not the other way round; that's what I convinced myself.

Then, at fourteen, I was distracted by the attentions of an older man. I wonder now if she saw the signs and perhaps could have warned me, not that I would have listened. Or at least told my father. What would he have done? I knew what he did two years later when I was pregnant at sixteen. My problems were many then and I never once thought my mother could help, since a bottle was never far from her lips.

'Is she okay from the fall?'

'Your mother fractured three ribs, Ms Flowers. Normally, we wouldn't keep her in because there's nothing to be done for fractures apart from painkillers and time to heal. But because of her dementia, we think she should stay here until the nursing home can arrange better facilities and support for her.'

'What if she came with me?'

The surprise added an unattractive sheen to his face.

'My understanding from speaking to the nursing home is that you haven't visited your mother in some time, Ms Flowers.'

'Ten years, not since the day they took her in.'

'So why now?'

Why indeed? Best to let him think it was guilt.

'We have some catching up to do.'

He considered that for thirty seconds. 'Okay. Why don't you speak to your mother while I talk to the care home?'

I nodded as he showed me into her room. She lay there sleeping and I knew I didn't dare wake her. As he went to make his call, I peered at my mother, wondering if her condition was in the genes, and my memory lapses and increased drinking had come from her.

I watched her for five minutes, seeing my face in hers before it got too much for me.

As I left, I worried this scene would play out again with Abbey staring at me in a hospital bed thirty years from now.

5 PANDORA: THE DATE

As first impressions go, it wasn't great. He was dressed entirely in sportswear, which was strange for a man in his forties. Unless he was some famous sports personality I was unfamiliar with. I scrutinised him up close; with the dirt under his fingernails and the extra chin threatening to hitch a ride on his chest, he appeared as far removed from sporting excellence as one could get. Still, he had the information I needed, and I'd put up with anything for that – even his aftershave, which smelt like a car on fire.

'I can see you're impressed with the clobber.'

He held out his arm for me to get a better look at his attire. I offered him my most delicate smile, one honed many years ago and not quite beaten out of me yet. I'd always found the pursuit of sport or leisure activities a curious thing. My time away from the city in the last decade had presented me with an opportunity to improve my fitness, but my earliest memories of sport at school were not good.

Physical exercise classes were one of those things only the masochistic enjoyed, and that was mainly the teachers.

Most of the kids, especially the girls, had such low opinions of their bodies, it was always an anxious time having to get changed in front of others, and then parade around in shorts or skirts which were too long or too short.

I was no different from most who appeared to suffer from body dysmorphia. Perhaps it resulted from staring at images and videos of the bold and beautiful that seemed to be everywhere. I remember getting the bus to school one day, gazing at the advert along the route proclaiming the best beach body for a woman was large breasts, thin hips, and legs long enough to reach the stars. And that was the message I got, that I needed to look like the women I saw in the magazines to achieve something in life. It didn't matter if you did well at school, not if you came from my background since it would restrict your opportunities.

The memories scuttled back into the shadows as I studied my date. He wasn't overweight, but his baggy clothes and the way he slouched into the chair made him look like a jelly ready to explode. His beard and hair reminded me of a Leonardo Di Caprio movie I'd seen, and I half-imagined he'd wrestled a bear to get here.

One of the bar staff brought a pint of Magners for him and a double gin and tonic for me. I'd had my eye on the sherbet lemonade flavour for ages and thought this was the perfect time for it. It was just the right mixture of sweetness and strength as I sipped it. As we sat in the corner of the empty pub, he reached into his pocket and removed a packet of biscuits; they were *Wagon Wheels*. He offered me one. I declined. He bit into his with relish.

'Pub grub is always so expensive, so I bring my own, as long as none of the staff sees me.'

I glanced at the menu as I nodded at him, noticing you

could get steak and chips with extra onion rings, plus a pint of beer or glass of wine, for less than four quid.

'You never said you were this clever on your profile, Darren.'

Bits of chocolate stuck to his teeth as he grinned. 'Aye, well, I had to keep some secrets to make the rest of the night interesting, didn't I?' He glanced over his shoulder. 'Is this the first time you've done online dating?'

I bit through a chunk of ice and let the alcohol warm my throat. 'It is. I haven't had access to the internet for a while.'

He finished his treat and struggled to contain a burp. 'Were you up in the Amazon or the desert?'

I nodded. 'Something like that.' The gin tasted like opening presents on Christmas Day. 'You said on your profile you'd been married before.'

Darren grimaced. 'Aye, not something I want to remember, but I thought it best to be honest.'

'Not the happiest of times, then?'

He finished his pint and the *Wagon Wheels* at the same time. 'She wasn't a bad lass, just very boring.' He winked at me. 'I think she feared getting naked, if you know what I mean.'

'Are you still in touch?'

He removed his phone to order another round through his app.

'Nah, we've nothing to talk about. She went up in the world and moved to the new estate when we split.'

I took a ten-pound note from my purse. 'Here, use this for the drinks and keep the change.'

He grabbed it without protest. 'See, I knew you were a good sort. Most of the lasses round here never put their hands into their pockets, always wanting you to get the booze or the takeaway with nothing in return.'

'Where she lives, is that the Beckett Estate over the other side of the bridge?'

'That's the one. A ten-minute walk from here, but I never visit her.'

'But you know where she lives?'

He moved forward and grabbed my hand. His flesh was lizard-like and I had to refrain from flinching.

'Don't be jealous, love; the ex means nothing to me now.'

I allowed him to continue rubbing his thumb against my palm.

'You can't blame me, though, can you, Darren? What if I see you walking into one of the houses on that estate? I won't know if you're seeing her again or not.'

He squeezed my fingers. 'Darling, I guarantee I'll never set foot inside 35 Hawkeye Terrace. Now let's enjoy these drinks and see where the night takes us, eh?'

Half an hour later, it took me outside while he was in the toilets. I deleted my fake online dating account as I left. I'd uploaded no photos, so I didn't have to worry about anyone recognising me. Darren was so clueless, I guessed he wouldn't be able to remember much about the woman who stood him up tonight.

I'd got what I'd come for, with the added pleasure of the gin. Of course, I'd have to scrub my hands in hot water when I got home to remove his stink from me, but it was worth it. Tomorrow night, 35 Hawkeye Terrace would have an unexpected visitor.

6 JEN: THE MEMORIES

I collected Abbey and Francine after their meal. I didn't
get out of the car, staying in to avoid Beth Rigsby trying
to promote my daughter into professional football, though
she must have mentioned it to them during their celebration
banquet.

'What do you think of Abbey playing for Chelsea, Ms
Flowers?'

Francine spoke while eating a slice of pizza, the smell of
cheese and garlic settling on me like a heavy carpet.

'What about your musical careers, girls?'

I pulled the car away from the restaurant and drove
towards Francine's house to drop her off. I'd yet to meet her
parents, but she didn't seem bothered by it.

Abbey leant over from the back to stare at me.

'We can do both, Mum. The Orchestral Musical Girls
will continue even when I play football.'

'The Orchestral Musical Girls? I thought you were
called Diamonds and Pearls?'

'Nah.' Francine dropped bits of cheese on the floor. 'We
needed a name change to match the new music.'

'You're not a rock two-piece anymore, in the manner of The White Stripes?'

'Oh, Mum. We've grown and developed since then. We're an electronic duo now: OMG.'

She slumped into her seat and stole pizza from her mate. I was pleased they both had the music and the football, but was concerned Abbey might overdo it. It was good she had ambition, but her schoolwork was still the most important thing. She had two years left to work towards her exams and think about college and university.

I took Francine home, noticing she'd added more makeup to her face, with the kohl rimmed under her eyes covering most of her cheeks.

'Is Francine obsessed with cosmetics, Abbey?'

She'd climbed into the front seat.

'Oh, it's nothing, Mum. She just enjoys messing around with makeup. Didn't you at her age?'

'Not that I remember.'

'Well, it was a long time ago, and your memory is terrible now.'

'No, it isn't.'

'Yes, it is. Only yesterday, you forgot the cat's name.'

'Rufus? I didn't forget his name.'

Abbey opened the window to discard some pizza she'd picked from her teeth.

'You called him Rattus.'

I shook my head. 'That was a joke, love.'

'Last week, you forgot I had band practice on Wednesday nights.'

I drove slower than usual, my brain working in synchronicity with the car's speed. She was correct; I had forgotten. But I'd done a fourteen-hour shift at work, so I put it down to that.

'Perhaps I wanted you to stay at home with me that night.'

She placed her hand on my arm. 'Oh, Mum, are you feeling lonely in your old age? You should be like Jack and do some online dating.'

'What do you know about that?'

Abbey laughed out loud. 'Have you seen that girl he's knocking off?'

'Abbey! Don't be so crude. And she's a young woman, not a girl.'

She bent herself double with laughter. 'She's a very young woman, is that Tiffany. She's only a few years older than me, and he's as ancient as you.'

I wanted to argue with her about Jack's love life, but I couldn't because she was right.

'What do you know about Jack's romantic adventures?'

She winked at me. 'Nothing gets past us girls, Mum; you should know that.'

As I parked outside the house, thinking of Jack and what had happened to my mother, I wondered what I knew about those around me. Abbey bounded out of the seat and let herself in. She was upstairs and in the shower before I could lock the front door. I went to the kitchen and opened the fridge, the bottles of Desperado calling to me. My hand shook as I ignored the alcohol and grabbed a can of Coke instead.

I hadn't eaten for most of the day, but the rumble in my stomach wasn't because of hunger. Could I visit my mother without telling Abbey what was happening? I considered the question and retired to the living room, turning on the TV to find something mindless to fall into. Abbey was singing upstairs, not anything I recognised, so I guessed it was one of her new tunes. Rufus strolled in and glared at me. I raised my can to the furball.

'Don't you think Rattus is a much better name?'

The moggy crept away with a look of disdain on his face, and my thoughts returned to my mother and her condition. I got my phone and opened a web browser, searching for dementia stories. Most of the results focused on the causes and how to deal with them for patients and their families. That led me to a forum where people spoke about their experiences. Most posts were heart-breaking, but this was the worst:

I have a sneaking suspicion some commenters lambasting relatives for not looking after those with dementia at home have had no experience with such a person. We're into our third year of looking after my father-in-law, and on Thursday, he's going into respite care for two weeks, which has an option of extension for up to six weeks, depending on his assessment. We're all heaving a massive sigh of relief as he's gone from a dotty, fit man to an obsessive/compulsive who has come to the point of harming himself even when we're around. On the last occasion we let him go to the local shop on his own, he brought back some biscuits, which he handed to my daughter, complaining they were 'too hard and tasted horrible.' They were, in fact, dishwasher tablets. He did, however, enjoy the half-packet of dog treats he'd put in the same shopping bag.

He can no longer tell the time of day or night and gets up to all sorts of mischief at one in the morning when we're trying to sleep. He'll switch on every light in the house, the TV, and his heater in his room, even in summer, and when we get him into bed, he's up and starts again an hour later. Our power bills look like we just bought the London Eye. We have had to deadlock the doors to safeguard the place as he's let strangers in without our knowledge, mistaking them for family members. This has caused him to attack the doors with knives and other implements to force them open.

The situation is an exhausting, frustrating nightmare, and all we can do is hang on and hope to find safe long-term care for him. He's gone from a friendly man to a suspicious delusional who yesterday carried on a fifteen-minute conversation with several people in the empty car in our garage. My wife and I work and live in fear of returning to some serious incident at home.

I couldn't keep reading after that. Was it my future staring at me?

Abbey brought me crashing back into the present.

'Is Ray my dad?'

My father took me to church every week for six years, from ages ten to sixteen, until he discovered one of his friends in the congregation had got me pregnant. That's why I know there's no such thing as Hell; not in the biblical sense, anyway. Of course, there's the Hell many of us make for ourselves or others, but that has nothing to do with demons or devils. I'd skirted around the edges a few times in my life, but I'd never fallen into the abyss until Abbey repeated the question I always feared she'd ask.

'Is Ray my dad?'

Now I was in a Hell of my own making.

The TV screen was filled with politicians turning orange as they shouted at each other, so I thought I'd misheard her at first. Or I hoped I had.

'What?' I muted the sound and turned to her.

'Ray Simpson, the man you were married to for two years; is he my father?'

It wasn't the question about Ray that bothered me – I was surprised she even remembered him since she was three when I got married and five when the divorce came through – but the idea of her wondering about her father after all this time. I'd expected the question to come as she got older, but as every day passed with no interest from her in him, I relegated the subject to the darkest corners of my mind.

I did my best to appear calm, even though something resembling the hottest chilli beans in the world was holding a party inside my guts.

'What's brought this on, Abs?'

'Some girls from the team were talking about their dads, saying how they were glad their kids were playing football, and they asked me about him, my father.'

Over the years, I'd stockpiled many answers to the question of Abbey's biological line: he'd passed away; run off; joined the Foreign Legion; was in prison; met another woman; met another man; even been abducted by aliens. None of them seemed satisfactory.

'I didn't think you remembered Ray, love.' Who can recall anything from those early years?

She slumped into the sofa. 'I had forgotten him, mostly.' She glanced around the room. 'Especially since there aren't any photos of him or of the two of you.'

'It was a long time ago, Abbey. I don't like dwelling on the past.'

'Did you fall out of love?'

How could I tell her you can't fall out of love if you were never in it in the first place? I used the TV remote to switch channels, finding the *Father Ted* episode where he fixes the raffle to win a car.

'We just drifted apart. These things happen.'

'Is he my father?'

I kept on with the delaying tactics. 'This is because of the girls on the team?'

She put her hands on her knees. 'No, not only that. I saw him the other day.'

It was my turn to snap forward and drop the remote on my foot.

'Fuck!'

'Mum!' Abbey grinned at me as a thousand bolts of lightning shot through my toes.

'Feck, feck, feck.' I danced on one leg like a demented woman doing an Irish jig. The thought of my ex-husband only made the pain worse. 'Where did you see him? Did he speak to you? Did you talk to him?' He was supposed to be in Australia, sheep farming.

'He waved at me, that's all. It was during the game last week.' She peered right into me. 'The one you didn't go to.'

I sat and grabbed my throbbing foot, trying to squeeze out the agony.

'And you recognised him, after ten years away?'

'Yeah, he looks exactly the same.' She gazed at me. 'Though he doesn't look like me.'

There was no way around it now.

'That's because Ray isn't your father, Abbey. You were born three years before I met him.'

'But you were married?'

'Yes, for two years.'

Two interminably dull years where we both realised we had nothing in common, at least not enough to keep us together and bring up a child.

'So why aren't I called Abigail Simpson?'

'Because I didn't want to take his surname, and he wasn't bothered.'

'Good. Everyone at school would give me Hell for being

one of the *Simpsons*.' Her smile lessened the agony in my foot. 'And Flowers is a much better name.'

Father Dougal was getting insects mixed up with incense on the TV as I flexed my toes.

'Do you remember anything about my marriage, about Ray being around?'

'No, not really. I hadn't thought of him at all in years until I saw him, and then when the girls were talking about their dads, I started wondering about mine.'

'I'm surprised you haven't asked me about him before.'

She pushed her back into the sofa. 'I guessed you didn't want to talk about it and, well, I thought we were doing okay on our own. We didn't need anyone else in the house, did we?'

'No, love, we don't.'

I waited for a reply, yet she just sat there saying nothing. Noise drifted across from the TV, but there was only silence between us. Rufus strolled over and jumped into her lap. She stroked his chin, the purring adding an extra vibration to the rhythm echoing inside my head.

Did it make any difference if Ray was back in the country? No, not really. But why was he at the ground where Abbey's football team played? He'd shown no great desire to be her father when we were together, so surely he wouldn't be interested now?

I watched her play with the cat and wondered when she'd return to the truth about her father. And what would I tell her?

7 PANDORA: THE PRISON

My leg throbbed as the vodka and orange warmed the back of my throat. It was the day of the week I hated the most, and no amount of booze was going to change that.

I'd never liked Sundays; they always reminded me of prison too much. As I crawled out of bed, my fingers touched the wall, searching for some sensation to make me feel real. I closed my eyes and I was free, not locked in a cell the size of a closet, bits of my mind and soul stolen with every knock on the door, my privacy non-existent. In the dark, I was somewhere else, anywhere but there: running up that hill; dipping my toes in the sea; feeling my gut as the rollercoaster twisted and turned. And finally, listening to her voice, hearing her laughter.

It was a category A prison for women and young offenders, a sprawling place with room for six hundred inmates that featured a mother and baby wing where the children could stay after birth. On my first night inside, one prisoner gave birth alone in her cell. When the guards came the next day, the child was dead. They had an investigation, but nobody was held responsible.

The journey there was long, a thirty-year voyage for me, but the morning I arrived was an uncomfortable ride. Myself and ten others stuffed into a sweatbox driven by a bloke who must have believed he was auditioning for a part in one of those *Fast and Furious* films. Half the girls were sick before we reached our destination, a grand building which a guard later told me was built in the late Victorian age to contain those with mental health problems.

I received a new set of clothes on arrival, but not those lovely uniforms with arrows on them. A prison officer interviewed me to see if I was okay, which I thought a strange question since the judge had sentenced me to ten years of incarceration. The officer also offered me a five-minute phone call to let someone know where I was, but I declined. My daughter didn't need to know. She was safe with her father, or so I believed.

My first morning there, I went from my cell to the prison food servery unit and joined the queue. There were three guards on duty when the fight broke out behind me. I turned to see two women grappling on the floor, one of them covered in beans while the other tried to stab her through the eyes with a fork. Their screams and shouts cut through the air, but nobody flinched, not even the guards. That was how my everyday life would be from then.

And I'd hated beans ever since.

During my first week behind bars, my anxiety threatened to consume me. It unnerves you when you witness a woman having boiling water thrown in her face. I soon learnt that violence was everywhere, and it puts you on edge; say the wrong thing, or look at the wrong person, and you could be hurt and never offered medical treatment. I witnessed assaults all the time, guards using violence to constrain inmates or prisoner on prisoner attacks. And there were frequent sexual assaults, most of which went unreported.

As well as same-sex relationships, some female prisoners engaged in sexual favours with the officers to get drugs or food. It was normalised, often gossiped and giggled about.

Losing liberty, family, especially if you are a mother, and the violence and isolation led to many inmates planning self-destruction. Some would lose custody of their children over everything that had happened to them, and that's why they'd start self-harming because it was the only area where they had control. Usually, the self-harm was cutting arms, but people would swallow batteries or rub their skin off using whatever they could get their hands on. It was a cry for help, not attention.

Locked inside, you had to find a way of coping. For me, it was reading and focusing on getting out. And learning how the prison system was harsher on women than men.

Unlike me, most women were there for non-violent offences, often for crimes such as theft, handling stolen goods and non-payment of council tax. Imagine going to jail for not paying your tax – most of the rich people in the world would be behind bars if those rules applied to them.

Many women I met inside ended up receiving a short sentence that had a massive impact on them. If they were the sole carer for children, the kids would have to go with other family members, or the local authority would get involved if they weren't around. If you were in prison for eight weeks, you could lose your home because your access to support would change. If you were in custody, you could come out homeless with no benefits and find your children taken away from you.

It was punishment on top of punishment, designed to hurt those women caught up in the system. One incident should never define an individual. Most of the time, inmates were characterised by their crime, but it didn't define them. Some chose the wrong lifestyle or were brought up in dysfunctional homes, suffered domestic violence, drug addiction, or mental illness. All that was required was an intervention to get desperately needed help. Incarceration and excessive prison time are not always the answer. We all have redeemable qualities and deserve a second chance.

But being in prison does allow you to reflect upon your life. After inmates had served a short amount of time, I discovered they grappled with what they'd done. People go to prison and they're angry, and it's overwhelming. They come from chaotic backgrounds or are victims of trauma themselves. But in prison, they're forced into an organised system. Then, after a few years, they settle down and work on themselves. They have therapy and get educated, are given work and become the person they could have been with proper mentors or a decent education.

And I made my own discovery: the walls in your head are worse than those in your cell.

8 JEN: THE MOTHER

The nursing home was not what I'd expected. Fresh flowers filled the reception, the aroma lifting my fluttering heart. As I gave my details to the woman at the desk, she signalled for a staff member to take me to my mother. She led me into a large room where a group of residents enjoyed the entertainment provided by musicians and a choir.

My guide must have seen the shock on my face.

'The power of music, especially singing, to unlock memories and kick start the grey matter is a crucial feature of dementia care. This is because it reaches parts of the damaged brain in ways other forms of communication can't.'

My mother wasn't with the group, but I couldn't stop staring at their joy. A woman clutching a Zimmer frame was swaying from side to side with the music, while next to her, two men were busy moving their heads and shoulders to the rhythm. All the rest were clapping or singing along.

'They look like they're having a good time.'

My guide was also enthused. 'The brain's auditory

system is the first to fully function at sixteen weeks, which means you are musically receptive long before anything else. So it's a case of first in, last out for a dementia-type breakdown of memory.'

I was impressed with her knowledge. 'You're well trained in this.'

'Oh, yes, the management ensures everyone is up to date with the latest techniques for dealing with dementia.'

As she spoke, a musician moved into the middle of the residents and handed them some tambourines. It seemed risky to me.

'Aren't you worried they might throw the instruments at others?'

'No, definitely not. With these sessions, we aim to reach every person. What we don't want is musicians standing behind a stand. They have to be proactive and stimulating to keep the attention of this audience. We have one flautist who dances around the room like the Pied Piper.' She stepped closer to me. 'Some people here are quite far gone, with no language, no recognition. But if you sing hymns or Christmas carols or play music from their past, they come alive.'

'Where does my mother fit into this?'

Her eyes lost their sparkle as the whole group started singing along to *Bachelor Boy* by Cliff Richard.

'Ruth's dementia is severe. She has very little short-term memory. As a result, her behaviour is unpredictable and disinhibited, but she is spirited. She's thrilled by both using and hearing bad language. She's incontinent and has reduced mobility. However, she enjoys her food and, having regressed to being a young woman in the prime of life, has an overriding desire to find a mate and is not shy in telling everyone about it.' Her smile returned. 'You must look forward to seeing her after all this time.'

How could I reply to that? With a part truth.

'It has been too long.'

She continued to grin as she led me from the singing and down a corridor. More flowers lined the space, and an array of framed paintings of the countryside were hanging on the walls. If I didn't know why most people were there, I might have thought it was a nice place to live.

'Here's Ruth's room.' She knocked on the door. 'She knows you're coming, so I'll leave you two alone.'

She returned to the music and left me standing there, holding my breath before I saw my mother for the second time in twenty-four hours; and the second time in a decade. And then I heard her voice.

'Come in.'

My fingers trembled as I touched the door, the chill of the wood surging through my hand and up my arm. It continued travelling, infecting every part of me until my legs froze on the floor. A lifetime of insecurities threatened to overwhelm me until instinct kicked in and I entered.

She sat on the bed facing me, a copy of the Bible in her hands, the leather cover mimicking the flesh on her face. I recognised it from my youth.

'Hello, Mother.'

Would she recognise me? Would she remember what happened in our family?

'Take a seat, Jennifer; we've got a lot to talk about.'

I slipped into the single sofa opposite the bed, glancing at the artwork on the walls, trying to recall where I knew the vivid watercolours from. I watched her and wondered if she remembered I hated being called Jennifer.

'How are you, Mother?'

She grinned and tapped the side of her head. 'I'm going mad, Jennifer. That's why I painted those pictures. Don't you recognise them?'

I stared at them again, delving into my memories to resurrect those places she'd recreated in art.

'They're the views from the back of our house, where it looked upon that vast field the council built houses on.'

'Yes, they are. You used to play there with your father. Do you remember?' I moved my head slowly and nodded. 'That was until you tricked poor Bob into sleeping with you.' She shook her head. 'Are you still a dirty girl, Jennifer?'

I resisted the urge to stand and leave. 'I was sixteen and Robert Green was forty, Mother. Don't you see anything wrong with that?'

Her eyes narrowed and darkness descended. 'Who are you? Why are you in my room?' Her voice increased in volume as her lips trembled. 'I'm going to call the police.'

Then an idea struck me. I removed my ID card and showed it to her.

'I am the police, Ruth. I'm here because I need your help.'

I went to the bed and sat next to her, thinking I'd feel nothing for the woman who'd felt nothing for me. But it was impossible. My heart thumped against my ribs, ready to burst.

'Have you seen your husband recently, Mrs Flowers?'

She squeezed my hand. 'Oh, Inspector, call me Ruthie. Mark always calls me that.'

Not when I was around. Or had I forgotten that?

'Does he visit you?' I couldn't call her Ruthie. The word would have stuck to my teeth.

'Oh, yes. He comes every day.' She stared at a spot on

the wall. 'He should be here soon. You can wait and see him.'

I jumped up with a start, tearing myself away from her so the bed wobbled, and so did she. She was about to hit the floor when I grabbed her arm and steadied her. She was skin and bone beneath those clothes, not the sturdy woman I remembered. But how much did I remember? If he was visiting every day, perhaps he had left that message for me. He'd said he wanted to talk about my mother. As she regained her balance, I regained mine in my head.

'When Mark comes here, Ruth, does he bring your daughter, Jennifer?'

She raised fingers to her cheek. 'Goodness, no. Jenny disappeared years ago.'

My hand shivered on her arm. 'What do you mean, disappeared?'

She pulled from me and crossed her arms, her mouth forming a wrinkled scowl.

'The girl took our little Jenny from the hospital.'

'What girl?'

She pointed at me. 'The one standing near you, her with the red hair and red dress and red shoes. She snatched my little girl, and we never saw her again. Jenny was the first baby kidnapped from a UK maternity ward. That's what the police told Mark and me. But you can ask the girl; she's right next to you.'

I stared into the space, expecting to see a ghost, but the only spirits in the room were the ones I was thinking about drinking as soon as I left. My mother was clearly hallucinating, but I didn't feel better about her false memories of me.

I stood to go. 'Thank you for your time, Mrs Flowers.'

'You don't believe me, do you?' She inched off the bed and moved towards me. 'You think I'm making it all up?'

Something manic lurked in her eyes and it was as if I was thirteen again, waiting for her to scream and shout as she swung the whisky bottle over her head. There was no worry she'd ever drop it – no matter what terrible state she was in, she'd never waste alcohol. I pushed the image into the shadows and wished for the woman who'd brought me here to return and rescue me.

'I believe you, Mrs Flowers.' I assumed she thought it was the truth.

She wagged her finger at me and the memories flooded back in waves, so fast I had to slump into the chair. Whenever she told me off, that was what she did: wag her finger so close to my face that one wrong move would have taken my eye out. This was before the drinking started and she pushed me aside as an inconvenience. The finger kept on moving as the spit drooled over her lips.

'No, you don't. I can see it in your empty eyes. A girl in red snatched from us our Jenny. There was a witness. He told the police. And we never found either of them.'

Her face glazed over as she returned to the bed. I didn't know whether or not to humour her. Could I make her condition worse if I said something to encourage this fantasy? Would it make her worse? Was that even possible?

'Are you telling me you don't have a daughter, Mrs Flowers?'

She'd hardly acted as if I was her child when I was there, so it wouldn't surprise me if the dementia had erased me from her life; my disappearance from her thoughts had happened a long time before that.

Her confusion switched to irritation in an instant.

'We got another Jennifer from the adoption agency. But she wasn't the same as our Jenny. She was terrible.' She peered straight at me, recognition and distress mixed in her face.

My heart was ready to give up, vibrating at a thousand beats per second. I was about to speak when a bell rang outside. My mother sprang from her bed as my guide returned.

'Time for tea and biscuits, Ruthie.'

She didn't need telling again, moving past me. She was gone before I could say anything. The nurse, or whatever she was, must have seen my startled expression.

'Your mother can move when she wants, can't she?'

I stopped her before she left. 'Does she have any visitors?'

She shook her head. 'Ruthie? No, only you. I've been here as long as she has, and you're the first. It's a shame because, on her good days, she can be very spirited. Was this one of her good days?'

I ignored the question. 'Does she hallucinate as well as having memory problems?'

She furrowed her brow. 'No, not really. If they have an infection, sometimes, residents will hallucinate, but I've never known that with your mother.'

'She told me she saw a red-haired girl standing next to me.'

'Oh. No, that's new. Perhaps seeing you after such a long time triggered a memory.'

It had triggered something. Someone screamed at the other end of the corridor, and a trickle ran down my spine. I'd visited the worst examples of humanity inside prison cells. Yet now, in this idyllic setting, I felt as if I was trapped in a Thomas Harris novel. I expected the staff member to sprint off in the howl's direction, but she continued to gaze at me.

'I suppose that's possible.' Then, against my better judgement, I asked her something I thought I'd never hear myself say. 'Can I revisit her?'

She put her hand on my arm and led me to the reception.

'Of course, Mrs Flowers. If you give me your phone number, I'll get one of the admin team to call you about visiting hours.'

I wrote my mobile details on the back of my police card, hoping the Met name and address might provide some influence later if I needed it. Then I left with my mother's words ringing in my ears.

Jenny disappeared years ago.

9 PANDORA: THE REDEMPTION

Getting into the house was always going to be the hardest part. But Darren had whispered a little nugget to me before I'd abandoned him – his ex-wife Betty was a born-again Christian. So all I needed was a few Jesus pamphlets in my hand and I assumed there would be no problem; once I sorted out the dark glasses and wig. I'd checked out the estate where Betty lived online enough to know there were no CCTV cameras, but I wouldn't run the risk of anyone seeing me and giving the police a description once I'd finished.

But I needn't have worried about that as darkness engulfed me as I arrived. Most of the streetlights were broken, while others flickered in and out in the rain. Everywhere smelt of dog shit. It didn't take long to reach her house, the building separated by gaps on either side. I fixed my best false smile and knocked, the damp staining my fingers.

'Hello, can I help you?'

Her voice drifted through the wood before she opened the door. My teeth ached as I smiled.

'Have you invited Jesus into your life?'

Betty's grin was as big as her eyes, making her resemble a demented toad. She grabbed my arm before I could stop her.

'Please come in and tell me all about it, dear.' If I'd wanted to protest, which I didn't, she didn't let me. Instead, she pushed me into the living room and the first available seat. 'Would you like a cup of tea?' I shook my head. 'How about something stronger, then?' She moved towards a cabinet next to the TV.

'No alcohol has ever passed my lips, Mrs...?'

She sat opposite me. 'Call me Betty. And you're right about the booze. God forbids it, I know, but sometimes I fall into temptation.' She peered up as if looking for the Almighty above her. 'I guess we all need something to help with our redemption.'

I watched her clutch at the cross around her neck, glancing over the room for any other religious iconography, but surprised to find none. She held a hand out to me. I thought she wanted me to shake it until realising she wanted to look at the leaflets I'd picked up outside King's Cross.

'You probably know what's in here by heart, Betty.'

She took them from me.

'You never know, dear; there's always something new to learn.' She buried her face in the pages and scanned through them. 'Fundamental to the message of the New Testament is the announcement that Jesus of Nazareth is the fulfilment of Israel's messianic hope and that, in him, the long-awaited redemption has arrived. Deliverance of humankind from its state of alienation from God has been accomplished through the death and resurrection of Christ. In the New Testament, redemption requires a price paid, but the plight that demands such a ransom is moral, not material. Humankind is held in the captivity of sin from which only the atoning death of Jesus Christ can liberate.'

'And what do you need redeeming from, Betty?'

She dropped the leaflets at her feet. I bent my knees to pick them up.

'That's a difficult question, dear. First, I'll have to get to know you better.' She smiled at me through yellowing teeth. 'What's your name?'

'I am Pandora, newly released from my box.'

She laughed at me like an adult listening to a child say something stupid.

'Pandora wasn't in the box, dear. She had the box and opened it to let Evil into the world.'

She pronounced evil with a capital E.

'Is that what you believe?' I said.

'Well, some Bible scholars identify Pandora with Eve and claim all the world's problems stem from her.'

'So you think women are to blame for everything bad in the world?'

Her laugh swept dust from the arm of the chair. 'Perhaps not all of them, but we have to know our place in this world according to God's law and never sway from it.'

'Pandora never had a box, Betty. It was a jar she held, much like this one.'

I removed the container from my coat and showed it to her. Her confusion was a joy to behold.

'What's that? It smells funny.'

I unscrewed the top. 'Some would say it's the elixir of life.'

She pulled back from me, her face screwed up into a parody of *The Scream*.

'Why have you got petrol in there?'

I smiled as I glanced at her sparse belongings.

'This isn't the first time someone has sat before you like this, is it, Betty?'

She placed one hand on her chest and I hoped she wasn't having a heart attack.

'What... what do you mean?'

'You live frugally on this terrible estate, but I suppose you have to since you took early retirement without a pension. Your benefits will only go so far.'

I reached for the coffee table between us and lifted the photo album towards me. Betty's fingers flickered against her dirty blouse, and for one second, I assumed she'd try to stop me before she thought better of it.

'Leave that alone; it's private property.'

I ignored her and flicked it open. 'You've got some lovely holiday photos here, Betty. Australia, Jamaica, Barbados, Florida, Hawaii. And that's only from the last eighteen months. I bet you have older ones in the house somewhere, don't you?'

Her face was one long, tortured shadow. 'Who are you?'

'I told you. My name is Pandora.'

'What do you want?'

'Information, that's all.' I removed the lighter from my pocket and placed it next to the jar of petrol on the coffee table. 'There'll be no trouble if you give me what I want.'

She sank further into the chair. 'What could you possibly want from me? I'm a sixty-year-old woman with no job, no family, and no friends.' She peered behind her. 'There's fifty quid in the top drawer. You can have that.'

It was my turn to laugh. 'No, Betty, I don't need your money.' I pointed at her face. 'I have to pick your brain about your former job.'

'My job? I worked for social services all my life.'

'Yes, I know.' I lifted the lighter and ran my fingers over the cracked metal. 'You were a social worker for forty years.' I shook my head. 'You must have seen some terrible things.'

She relaxed a little in her seat. 'It was a difficult career, but a rewarding one.'

'I bet it was.' The flame sprang from the lighter as I flicked the switch. 'So what was it that made you stop protecting children? Was it the money or the threats against you?' The yellow light flickered warmth over my skin. 'I suppose it was a mixture of both, wasn't it?'

Betty's fear had vanished, her eyes flickering red with defiance.

'I don't know what you're talking about. Now get out of my house before I call the police.'

She grabbed a mobile phone from the pocket of her tattered cardigan. There were soup stains down the front of it, and I wondered how old they were.

'You stopped protecting the children, Betty. I know you did, so don't lie to me. Give me his name, the one who led the abusers; the man who bought you off and threatened to set you on fire.' I unscrewed the top of the jar. The gasoline smell was intoxicating and reminded me of a drug den I'd frequented in Glasgow. 'You've got many secrets, Betty, but I only want that one. Just his name. Then I'll leave, and you'll never see me again, I promise.' It was a lie. 'It will be your redemption.'

She shrank into herself before my eyes, a pathetic, shrivelled creature old before her time.

'Is this a test? Did he send you here to test me?'

'Perhaps.' I stood over her, ready to empty the container. 'Will you give me his name?'

She wiped the sweat from her forehead. 'I don't know

who he is. I only told one person what happened, I promise.'

As a single tear dripped from Betty's eye, I believed her. But I needed that name, and it looked like she wouldn't provide it without some persuasion. So I administered some.

The petrol aroma bounced up to my nose as I emptied the jar. I thought Betty would scream, shout, or at least move, but she didn't. And then I remembered she'd experienced this before, ten years ago. She'd walked away from it then.

But she wouldn't now.

I set the Jesus pamphlets alight. Then she blurted out what I needed to know.

But it was too late then, both for her and me.

10 JEN: THE FIRE

'You told me Grandma was dead.'

I was still cleaning the water from my ears after the shower, but Abbey's words were like a thunderstorm in my head.

'Good morning to you as well.'

She pointed at the answering machine. 'You should listen to that.'

I did as instructed.

'Hello, Mrs Flowers. This is Rosewood Nursing Home regarding your mother, Ruth. After your visit yesterday, her memory appears to have improved, and she hopes you'll return to see her again. Ruth says she has something important to tell you. Thank you.'

'Well?' Abbey stood opposite me with hands planted on her hips, looking a lot older than fifteen.

'Let me grab a cup of coffee, and then I'll tell you all about it.'

My head was clearer by the time we were sitting in the living room, but her expression was still dark. I wondered if the pain in my skull was because I hadn't had a drink last night. In the last month, I'd found I couldn't get to sleep without one or two glasses of wine. Abbey had made the odd joke about me turning into an alchie, but I'd laughed it off. But I wasn't laughing now as she scowled at me.

'I'm waiting, Mother.'

It wasn't even Mum anymore.

'I was on my way to see your grandmother yesterday when the nursing home informed me she'd had a fall and was in the hospital. So I visited her while you were celebrating with pizza.'

I sipped at my coffee and waited for her volcano to explode.

'You told me my grandparents died in a plane crash before I was born.'

The drink curdled in my stomach. 'I don't think that's right, Abbey.'

She shook her head. 'It is.'

I put the mug on the table. 'You were only young when they left, two or three years old. They went to live abroad.'

The glare in her eyes told me she didn't believe that.

'And you never kept in touch?'

Was now the time to tell her how unloving my parents were, at least towards me? Or about my pregnancy and abortion at sixteen? Or my mother's descent into alcoholism before that? Or even how I now believed her early onset of dementia might have caused the drinking?

No, it wasn't.

'Parents and their kids sometimes grow apart, love.'

'And they never wanted to see me?'

How to answer that question? I moved over to take her hand, but she pulled away.

'That's just the way it was, Abbey.'

'I don't even know their names, my grandparents.'

I snapped back into the sofa. 'Ruth and Mark.'

'How old are they?'

'Sixty and sixty-three.' If he was still alive.

Confusion covered her face. 'Why is she in a nursing home at sixty?'

'She has dementia.'

'Isn't that young for someone to have dementia?'

'It can affect all ages, Abbey.'

And it was possible it could have been passed to both of us. I'd spent weeks researching the prospect, uneased by what I'd found. Studies of family history said if you have a close relative diagnosed with Alzheimer's, the most common form of dementia in older adults, your risk increased by about thirty per cent. I didn't know what type of dementia my mother had, but I'd discovered that Frontotemporal dementia was more likely to run in families and have a genetic link than other more common causes of dementia.

'That's terrible, Mum.' She got up, came around the table, and sat next to me. 'We have to visit her, both of us.'

She wasn't wrong. I had no right to keep Abbey from forming a bond with her grandmother, but I needed to speak to my mother alone before that.

'We will, love, but I need to see her on my own first. She was quite confused yesterday.'

Confused enough to see an imaginary girl in red standing next to me and claim she stole her baby from the hospital, and I was, well, what? Was I adopted to replace her stolen Jenny?

'Confused how?'

'She was just very absent-minded, forgetting who I was.'

Abbey narrowed her eyes. 'Maybe that's because she hasn't seen you for years.'

The bitterness in her voice slithered into my heart and stuck a knife there.

'You're right, love, but in her condition, I guess it will be a bit of a shock seeing us after all this time.'

My words appeared to soften her stance and she grabbed my hand.

'Of course, Mum.' She gripped my fingers. 'What happened to my grandfather?'

Well, apart from thinking he'd left a message on our answering machine a few months ago, I didn't know where he was. Not that I could tell her that.

'I don't know, Abbey. As soon as he put your grand-mother into the home, he was off.'

I hadn't thought about him until my mind started playing tricks on me.

'But you're a police inspector; you could find him, couldn't you?'

As I struggled to answer that, I was saved by my mobile ringing. I glanced at the screen and stood.

'I'll have to take this, love; it's Jack.'

She pulled away from me, got up, and left the living room as I answered the phone.

'I'm running a bit late, Jack, but I'll be there soon enough.'

'Late night?'

Was it? I couldn't remember.

'No, just a difficult conversation with Abbey.'

'Is everything okay?'

'Yeah, I'll tell you about it later. What's up?'

'There's no need to go to the station. We've been asked to go to the scene of a house fire.'

'Is it arson?'

'From what I can gather.'

'Were there people inside?'

'Looks like it. I'll send you the address and meet you there.'

He ended the call as I stared at the surrounding emptiness. The sounds of Abbey playing the keyboard drifted down from her room. I got up, grabbed my coat and car keys without saying goodbye. A maudlin version of *Tainted Love* escaped from Abbey's bedroom window as I left.

THIRTY MINUTES LATER, I parked in Hackney. It wasn't hard to find the scene of the crime. The smell of burning wood lingered in the air and, as I approached the damaged building, I was sure there was a faint trace of cooked human flesh in there as well. A group of dogs ran past me as a familiar face dealt with the curious onlookers.

'Is Detective Inspector Monroe here, Constable Sutton?'

She pointed towards the gap between the house and the one next door. A cursory glance told me it had avoided the fire so close by.

'He's with Ms Temple, ma'am.'

I nodded thanks and headed for my partner and the Met's Head of Forensic Science. The closer I got, the more the smoke aroma settled into my lungs. I saw the two of them dressed in protective clothing, with their shoes covered. Athena Temple held a set out to me.

'Detective Inspector Flowers, how nice of you to join us.'

I didn't take the protective clothes from her. 'Do I need to go inside, Athena?'

She pulled at the cloth near her forehead. 'Only if you don't want DI Monroe to come with me by himself.'

I couldn't tell if she was implying it would be a dereliction of duty on my part or that she'd get up to something she shouldn't with my partner. And then I remembered Tiffany. So I took the uniform and looked at him.

'What are we waiting for?'

He nodded to the right, where a fire service crew gazed at the blackened house.

'The Fire Investigation Officer in charge will take us inside to show what the Fire and Rescue Services have found.'

I struggled to get my leg into the protective uniform, thinking I'd put on weight since the drinking started, not to mention the nightly takeaway food. When was the last time I'd cooked a meal that hadn't come out of a microwave?

'If this happened last night, why are we only here now?'

'Because we didn't know it was foul play then.'

As the Fire Investigation Officer joined us, I pictured Fireman Sam and his moggy, which led me to think of our cat. Abbey had been right and I had forgotten Rufus's name. Jack introduced me to the FIO, Andy Greenham.

'What makes you believe it's foul play, Andy?'

'I'll show you.'

He led the three of us inside. There wasn't much damage to the entrance, only slight burning to the wall closest to the door. The aroma was more intense, settling on me like a blanket. I peered at the untouched carpet and stairs.

'Was the fire contained?' I guessed it must have been not to migrate outside of the house.

'Yes, but not by us. It didn't reach upstairs or into the

back.' He nodded towards the dark shell of the living room door. 'That's where it did all the damage.'

I took a deep breath and followed him in. The curtains had gone up in flames as the fire spread across the walls and into the ceiling.

'There's no damage upstairs?'

'Very little. But we have to be careful about what's above our heads. We've checked upstairs, and most of the house's structure, including the wooden beams and joists, is intact, but there's no telling if they've been weakened or not. Once we've finished here, the place will need a complete renovation or destruction.'

A two-seater sofa had burned into the carpet, with the TV next to it melted into a heap. It looked like a gruesome sculpture of metal and plastic constructed by Salvador Dali. But there was a worse sight in front: a human body, bent as if fighting in a boxing match, with all the flesh burnt away.

Jack approached the remains first.

'Is this the owner?'

The Fire Officer nodded. 'Betty Green. She'd lived here on her own for twelve years.'

I knelt where her feet should have been, the carpet and wood scorched around her.

'No one else in the house?'

'No,' he said.

I glanced over at the destruction. 'What makes you think this was arson?'

He bent down to my level. 'We evaluated everything last night, taking photos and videos, so there's a record of the original state of the scene. This area around the victim is the point of origin, what we call the seat of the fire. It's petrol. We thought she might have spilt it somehow, but we've searched and there's no container. The region where a fire starts will burn for longer, thus becoming the area with the worst destruction. Fires burn upwards; therefore, the seat of the fire is likely to be found at a lower point of burn damage, which is what we have here.'

I ran a gloved hand over the stain. 'How was it lit?'

'We checked all the usual suspects. The electricity is fine, and there are no gas appliances in the house. So sniffer dogs were brought in and detected the petrol as the accelerant, and paper residue was discovered in the ash at the victim's feet.'

We got up together.

'Could she have done this herself?' Jack said. 'Poured the petrol on the carpet, and then disposed of the container before returning here?'

'I suppose it's possible. That would explain why the fire localised here and never damaged the rest of the house.'

Jack glanced at me. 'Which would make it suicide?'

Greenham stared at us both. 'It seems unlikely, but I guess that's why you two are here.'

'Indeed.' But I couldn't see how we'd get much from the scene. 'Will you send all the photos and videos to our office?'

'It's already done, Inspectors. I emailed the material this morning.'

I thanked him and led the others from the property, the three of us standing outside in the drizzle, looking like giant condoms. The slight rain didn't cool me down, but it felt good to remove the protective clothes.

'What do you think, Athena?'

'I can only hope our victim passed out from the smoke before her flesh burnt.'

I folded the uniform. 'She looked bent over as if she was praying.'

'Or fighting,' Jack said.

Athena seemed keen to talk about it. 'The fire will have caused the soft tissues to contract, which forced the skin to tear and the fat and muscles to shrink. As a result, the internal organs will also have shrunk. In addition, the muscles contracted because of burning, which caused the joints to flex. As a result, burned bodies are often contorted into what's known as a pugilistic or boxer pose.'

I handed the uniform to her. 'Would the heat or the smoke have stopped her from resisting?' I couldn't understand why she'd stayed in the chair. 'Or could she have been restrained?'

'If she was, it will show up in the report from the Fire and Rescue Services.'

'Okay, thanks, Athena.'

We left her to finish with her team. I took in a huge breath, trying to clear the taste of ash and death in my throat. Then I strode over to Constable Sarah Sutton, who had been joined by Constable Jackie Grealish. Both of them had started training to be detective constables, something Jack and I had encouraged them to do. It was a two-year Detective Degree Holder Entry Programme and they seemed to have taken to it with relish, though I hadn't had much time to speak to either of them about it in the last few weeks.

'How is the homework going, ladies?'

Sutton grinned, but Grealish grimaced.

'I'm enjoying it, ma'am,' Sutton said.

'There's too much written work,' Grealish added. 'I prefer practical police work.'

'That's good, Constable Grealish, because I want the two of you to go door to door and speak to as many neighbours as possible to get background information on our victim, Betty Green.'

They went about their task as Jack and I got into my car. He strapped on his seatbelt.

'What now, Jen?'

'Just the usual. We trawl through the data and see if we can find why someone burnt a sixty-year-old woman alive.'

'My money is on an ex-husband or boyfriend.'

I didn't take the bet, switching the radio on instead. A shiver ran down my spine as *Tainted Love* drifted from the speakers, and I marvelled at the coincidence. And I didn't believe in coincidences. Still, it could have been worse.

It might have been *Light My Fire*.

11 PANDORA: THE AFTERMATH

Prison isn't about rehabilitation or redemption; it's a melting pot for extending your criminal knowledge and contacts. I first heard rumours about London's missing kids and who was responsible when I was locked up. In prison, I met a mother whose children were taken from her because of the social worker, Betty Green. She was the one who told me some of Green's secrets, which led me to others who knew of whispers and gossip about dear Betty. All I needed was her address since she'd gone to ground five years ago. She wasn't listed on the Electoral Register, and there was no internet footprint for the Betty Green I needed to see.

But there was the ex-husband, and experience had taught me that former partners never strayed too far from what they thought they owned. The police would speak to him; I knew that, but there was nothing he could tell them which would lead them to me, and that was if he even remembered much about Saturday night. My dating profile on the app was fake, but I'd deleted all the information and messages, anyway.

That's why I couldn't **control** my grin on the bus to work on Monday. The **headphones** warmed my ears, the sound of Nina Simone in **my head** a welcome relief from the kids' caterwauling **on the** way to school. I flicked through my book during **the journey**. This novel was many things, none good, new, or **enjoyable**. It was a thriller devoid of pacing or exciting language, a mystery bereft of clues, foreshadowing, or facts. **That made** it perfect for the journey, a place where I could **switch** off my mind to prepare for work.

This was my second **attempt with** the book, but the first time reading it. I'd listened **to it** as an audiobook during my imprisonment. Then, I'd **found** it engaging as the plot twisted and turned, jumping **from** scene to scene, back and forth in time. The writing **style was** rudimentary, but it kept me entertained. Yet, halfway **through**, I realised the iPod was on shuffle, and all the **chapters** were out of sequence. So now I had it as a paperback. **After** reading two chapters, I dropped it to the floor and **kicked it** under the seat.

Next to me was one **of those** free newspapers people always discard across the **city**. I picked it up and used it to remove the scarring on my **brain** from the book. It appeared to be full of strange but **true** stories from these sceptred isles: a woman fined after **walking** her husband on a lead and telling police he was **a dog**; a bodybuilder who went through a marriage ceremony **with** a sex doll; an egg fight in Tesco's after two women **argued over** who had the best tan; and, my personal favourite, **the story** of three creepy Victorian dolls strolling around **London** freaking people out on the Tube. It was just another **reason** not to use the underground. But there was **nothing** inside the paper about the death of the social worker.

I got off the bus a stop **before** the office, an hour before I was due at work. The excitement of yesterday meant I'd hardly slept last night, so I'd set off early and hoped it would reignite my brain cells.

Relight my fire.

Yes, I liked that term; terrible song, though – music for people who didn't like music; those who listened to Queen or the Foo Fighters. James Brown was feeling good inside my head as I took a seat in the park close to the office. I checked online for news of last night's fire, happy to read it hadn't spread to any other buildings. I may be a murderer, but I only intend to kill those who deserve it. And she did, the failed social worker, for her dereliction of duty and the wilful abandonment of the most vulnerable so she could earn thirty pieces of silver.

There was nothing to worry me in the news reports, no mention of witnesses or suspects. But then again, I didn't suppose the police would give such information away even if they had it. So I closed those sites and started a Google search: today's topic was missing persons in London.

One hundred and eighty thousand people are reported missing every year in the United Kingdom. Many are found, some are not. Those who are never located will have their case open for several years. The oldest open missing person's case on the Metropolitan Police books dates back to 1959. I didn't think they'd be found, just like Lord Lucan and that bloke from The Manic Street Preachers.

The latest reports included an autistic eighteen-year-old man; a pensioner with dementia; two teenage girls; and a father of four children – all had disappeared. I stared at their photos, read through their stories and those of the people they'd left behind. Their suffering seeped through the digital screen until I felt every agony they were going through.

I put the phone away as two women joggers ran past me, their laughter and joy contrasting to what I'd just read. Inside my jacket pocket lay a can of gin and tonic I'd purchased from the corner shop this morning. When I touched it, still concealed so none of the passers-by could see it, it was cold to the touch. A chill spread through my fingers, across my hand, and up my arm. I felt like Han Solo in *The Empire Strikes Back* as he was frozen in Carbonite.

'Are you okay, Mrs?'

A small child with saucers for eyes stood before me. For a second, I thought he was a ghost, some Victorian spirit sent to punish me for my crimes. Smoke and fire drifted from his mouth, my heart racing as I watched him peer into my soul. Then he sucked on a cigarette, and I had to restrain myself from telling him how bad it was for his health. Instead, I assumed the photo on the packet in his other hand of blackened dead lungs was warning enough.

'I'm fine, little boy. Shouldn't you be at school?'

I expected him to disappear in a wisp of the smoke coming from his lips.

'Nah, Mrs. School is for squids.'

He turned on his heels and ran into the park, his enigmatic words ringing in my head. Was squid one of those terms the youth of today used in a different context to adults?

I stood, resisting the urge to open the can and drink the gin, and made my way to work. Later on, during a lull in my tasks, I'd recheck the news to see if there was anything new about last night's flaming event. I'd taken my first step on the journey; now, I had to plan for the second.

12 JEN: THE HUSBAND

Betty Green was a ghost both online and in the real world. Sutton and Grealish's questioning of the neighbours hadn't yielded anything of use. Green kept to herself, rarely leaving her home apart from taking regular holidays. No one on the estate knew where she went; she always returned with a tan, but her passport must have gone up in the blaze as it wasn't in the house. As I went through the information the Fire and Rescue Services had provided, it seemed likely we'd find nothing useful from the crime scene regarding the culprit's identity. But was it murder?

Jack had no doubts.

'Perhaps she was a drug mule if she was going abroad three or four times a year.'

'A sixty-year-old ex-social worker?'

'Drug mules come in all shapes, sizes, and ages, Jen.'

I shook my head. 'That would mean she was involved with at least one criminal gang. How would they communicate with her if she rarely left the house?' The lack of CCTV on the estate was more than an inconvenience since we'd located no witnesses to Green's visitors that night. 'It would have to have been done online, and we found no computer or smartphone in her place.'

'The killer could have taken them with them,' Jack said.

'That's if somebody killed her.'

'It's ridiculous, really.'

I scrolled through the documents on the screen. 'What is?'

'Policing drugs in this country.'

It was time for his regular rant about those who make the laws we had to enforce.

'Go on, Jack, get it out of your system.'

'Drugs arrests can wreck the lives of otherwise decent, law-abiding people, and I think it's a disgrace that we, the police, arrest a person for possessing, for example, psychedelic mushrooms or some marijuana. Let's ignore drug use as long as there are no aggravating factors. I'd like to know precisely what harm anybody is doing if they smoke pot or take LSD in their own home. If these things were legal, there would be no criminal element whatsoever. It's madness.'

I didn't argue with him, returning my focus to the screen.

'I don't think this is about drugs, Jack. Of course, it's possible we didn't find a computer or phone because they were stolen, but the arson appears extreme for a burglary.'

'You think it was personal?'

My legs creaked as I stood. 'It seems the likeliest answer for now.'

As I flexed my knee to relieve the pain, Constable Sutton approached and handed me a piece of paper.

'We have a name and address for Betty Green's former husband, Darren.'

I took it from her and read the text.

'He lives five minutes from the crime scene.'

Jack got up and put his jacket on.

'Time to pay him a visit.' He nodded at me. 'I'll let you drive, but I'm still not ruling out the involvement of drugs.'

I grabbed my keys and considered what he'd said, feeling uneasy at my sudden urge for a glass of wine. And it wasn't even lunchtime.

MY STOMACH RUMBLED SO MUCH on the journey that Jack made me stop at a McDonald's drive-through. As I forced half a Big Mac into my mouth, he asked about my mother.

'How did she take seeing you again?'

Melted cheese dribbled over my lips. 'It was a mixture of confusion, distaste and lies.'

He stole some of my fries. 'Lies?'

I mentioned her claims about the stolen baby and that I was adopted.

'Jesus, Jen, you don't need all this stress.' I didn't argue. 'Does Abbey know of this?'

A slurp of Coke sent dizzying bubbles down my throat. 'No, I only told her a little about her grandmother. There'll have to be a meeting between them at some point. I'm not too fond of the idea, but it's not right for me to stop her from seeing my mother. Plus, she's asking questions about her father.'

'You never speak of him.'

'There's nothing to say. It was one night in my last term at university, and we've never been in touch since. I don't even know where he is. We were both drunk, but we knew what we were doing. So I'm not sure it's something I want to tell Abbey.'

'Life is never boring, is it?'

'And she's asking about Ray.'

'Your ex-husband?'

'That's him. She saw him recently in the crowd at one of her football matches.'

He ate more fries, chewing as he spoke. 'It never rains, but it pours, doesn't it?'

'It did at the match.' It was my turn to ask him some personal questions. 'Are you going to enlighten me about Tiffany?'

Jack rubbed his chin. 'What's there to say? It's fun for both of us, nothing more.'

'Are you sure? She seemed very keen the other day.'

He grinned at me. 'And why not? I'm quite the catch, you know.'

I finished the food and started the engine. 'I hope she has big hands.'

The laughter burst from him. 'You've watched too many *Carry On* films, partner.'

I laughed as well, pushing the thoughts of my mother, Abbey's father, and my ex-husband into the back of my mind, knowing they'd all return sooner rather than later. It was a different ex-husband we had to speak to now.

DARREN GREEN LET us into the house with no protest. His face was like a poorly boiled egg, all fractured and ready to break. Where he lived wasn't much better, the living room littered with empty cans and bottles, smelling as if someone had painted the walls with out-of-date curry. He offered us seats, but we didn't take them.

'Is this about Betty?'

His voice trembled over cracked lips, and I couldn't tell if the tears in his eyes were from the news of his ex-wife or his apparent hangover. The smell of alcohol hung over him like a cloud and tugged at my guts. Jack took out his notebook. I preferred to make notes on my phone, and then transfer them straight to the computer's case file, but my partner, as modern as he was, sometimes liked the old ways of doing things.

'When did you last see Betty, Mr Green?'

He didn't hesitate to answer. 'The day of the divorce, six years ago.'

Here was someone else who never contacted an ex, or so he was claiming. I glanced around the room, trying not to look at the stains on the carpet and the mildew on the walls.

'And you haven't kept in touch since?'

He slumped onto a shabby sofa and lit a cigarette. Another ancient craving leapt through my insides and I didn't have the heart to tell him to extinguish it. It was his house, after all. He sucked in a vast amount and blew it into the air. The smell reminded me of the corpse we'd seen close to here only a few hours ago – the body of his ex-wife.

'I saw her around a few times, coming out of the shops and that, but we never spoke. I don't think she ever noticed me.'

'But you knew where she lived?'

He twitched in his seat, his shoe catching on a discarded pizza slice near his feet.

'Yeah, I did. But I never went there.'

He peered at me before shifting his gaze into his lap.

Then he finished the cigarette, dropped it on the carpet, and lit another one.

'Where were you on Sunday night, Mr Green?' Jack said.

'The same place I go every night, the pub on the estate, the Hope and Grope. Speak to anyone in there, and they'll vouch for me.'

Jack put his notebook away. 'We will, Mr Green.'

I stared straight at Green, trying to fathom out what he was hiding.

'Do you know of any person who might want to harm your ex-wife?'

The cigarette wobbled between his lips, dropping ash on the carpet.

'Betty? She wouldn't hurt a fly, but there was... well, you know?'

'Know what, Darren?'

'Working for social services all that time, having to sign off on kids being taken away from their mums and dads, that was hard for her. And some of them, the parents, didn't take it very well. She was always getting threats. I think that's why she left when she did.'

Jack scribbled in his book. 'Do you know who any of these people are?'

Green shook his head. 'No, she wouldn't speak about them. She kept her job out of the house, but I knew what was happening. Sometimes she couldn't keep it all bottled up, and I'd come home to find her in bed crying. But she never wanted to talk about it.'

'Whose idea was the divorce?' I said.

He straightened his back on the sofa as if rediscovering his backbone.

'We just drifted apart, that's all.' He glared at me. 'It happens to a lot of couples.'

'Of course.' I turned to leave. 'We'll be in touch if we need a statement, Mr Green.'

He coughed like an asthmatic toaster, going up and down until he spat phlegm all over the carpet.

'There was something else that happened last weekend, on Saturday night.'

I stared at him as he shifted on the sofa. 'What was that, Darren?'

'Well, I was on this date with this lass, and she,' he rubbed at his throat, 'she asked me about Betty, wanted to know where she lived, said she needed to make sure I wasn't still seeing her, you know.' His cheeks had turned bright red. 'So, well, I thought nothing of it and told her the address, and then when I got back from taking a piss, she'd buggered off. And she never returned.'

Jack and I glanced at each other before my partner spoke.

'What was her name, Darren?'

He lit another cigarette. 'She said it was Cassie, but she's deleted all her details from the dating app where we met.'

I held out my hand. 'Can I look at your phone?'

'There's no point; I deleted the app as well. It's been a complete waste of time. She wasn't the first lass to mess me around, but at least she paid for a round of drinks.'

He reached across the sofa and got a packet of *Wagon Wheels*. He tore it open and stuffed one into his mouth.

'What did she look like?'

'Tall, a bit like you, fit, late thirties probably, with long dark hair and blue eyes.'

Jack scribbled some notes down while I asked Green a final question.

'Do you think this woman wanted to hurt Betty?'

He laughed as he replied. 'Nah, I can't see it. She was just checking if I was still messing about with Betty. Which I wasn't, since I haven't spoken to her in years.'

We finished up and left. Jack pulled his coat close to his chest.

'We better go to this pub to check his alibi.'

'And let's hope they had some cameras working there on Saturday night.'

'You think this Cassie could be our killer?'

I got in the car and pulled the seatbelt across me.

'She's the only lead we have. If there are working cameras in the pub, we might get a good look at her, if nothing else.'

But, of course, the Hope and Grope was devoid of any CCTV, working or not. So we weren't quite back at square one as we had this woman to find, and there was the possibility social services may have kept a record of any threats Betty Green had received from unhappy parents.

I guessed it was the first step on a long journey, but at least, if the killer were a disgruntled mother or father, there would be no more murders.

But I was wrong.

13 PANDORA: THE JOB

I tell strangers I work in an office. Only that. When they press for more information, I show them the deep lines on my hands, the large scar on my hip and, if they're lucky, the burn marks on my thighs. Most shuffle away after that, and I see the confusion in their eyes about what type of office it is and what job I do. Only one bloke tried to make a joke about it.

'You must use the most dangerous photocopier in the world.'

He had food stuck in his teeth and was missing the top of his little finger on the left hand. I suppose we could have bonded over the damage inflicted on our bodies, but his fondness for jazz music and the movies of Woody Allen turned me off. I soon shuffled him away and focused on my task.

I work in an office, doing the accounts for a small building firm. Most people leave me alone, but some over-step the mark sometimes. Maybe the long-time bricklayer who thinks the forty-year-old woman with the occasional black eye is an easy mark, or the young electrician who finds a spark in his loins for the woman he assumes might teach him something about being a man. They don't linger long when they see the mouldy bread I've used to make my sandwiches, or they smell last night's gin on my breath. Of course, their attention is unwanted, but it's still nice to be noticed once in a while.

The accounts don't take long, and the business owner, Bob, is unaware of how a computer works, so it's easy to pretend I'm working hard when I get the tasks done in half the time. I spend fifty per cent of my hours in the office doing crosswords online or trawling through various websites, annoying trolls.

It's a good job, considering how unemployable I was for a while. But Bob ignored my past. Perhaps he took a shine to me – or I reminded him of someone he knew – and he gave me the position halfway through my interview.

When I know nobody will visit the office, I listen to music or talk to my daughter. She always gives me recommendations for bands or albums. Based on her prompting, my current favourite is the Red House Painters; they cheer me up while I'm reading poorly written invective on the internet.

After work, I go to the local Aldi near my flat. It's cheap and cheerful and sells the best Californian wine available for under a fiver. Then it's a couple of glasses with a microwave meal before I settle for a night in front of the box, trawling through shows about conspiracy theories, impossible restaurants, or ancient aliens.

I don't speak to my daughter then, preferring to work on my plans for revenge.

The only time the phone rings is when someone is trying to sell me things or trick me into giving them my credit card details or my bank account password. I listen for about thirty seconds, perhaps a minute if I'm on the second glass of wine, before telling them I have their number and I'm going to track them down. They soon hang up.

But I don't mean it, of course. Outside of work, which is solitary, I never speak to anyone, so those calls might be the only conversations I have for days, especially over the weekend.

Still, the seclusion allows me to concentrate on what I have to do. My daughter tries to talk me out of it and tell me how dangerous it will be. I listen to her; how could I not? But nothing she says will change my mind. Revenge is everything to me now. The face I show to the rest of the world – to Bob and the others at work; to the stray men who speak to me on the odd occasion I go to the pub; to the people in the shops or on the buses – is only what I allow them to see. Underneath that face is the real me, the one who suffers isolation even when surrounded by people.

So I carry on doing the accounts, churning out the numbers while slipping a little extra into my electronic pocket, continue with the shopping and the drinking and the TV watching, all the while smiling so brightly nobody can see the darkness glittering underneath it all.

After the fire at Green's, I'd considered phoning in sick at work, but didn't. Staying in the flat all alone had no appeal to me for once. I'd still be on my own in the office, but I'd know there would be others just beyond the door. At least that's what I thought.

It was different when I got there.

As I entered, I knew something was wrong even before seeing the two uniformed police officers. Their backs were to me; they were speaking to someone I couldn't see. The breath vanished from my lungs as my heart crawled at my ribs, while the screaming in my head told me to get out.

I didn't know how the coppers had found me, but they had.

Then I heard a familiar voice.

'She's the best worker I've ever had, but she's also strange.'

'Perhaps she's on the spectrum.' That was Gladys, Bob's secretary.

'Sinclair Spectrum more likely.' The laugh was from Billy, one of the mechanics. He twisted his vocals into a perfect impression of a computerised human voice when he stopped laughing. 'I am Princess Pandora from the planet Metal Mickey, and I've come to conquer your world.' They all laughed together, even the coppers. 'Take me to your leader.'

They kept on laughing after I entered and stood behind the two police officers. Should I turn and run, get a head start before they could arrest me for the murder of the social worker? How did they know it was me? I was sure I'd been so careful, had left nothing behind and avoided any CCTV cameras along the route. But something must have gone wrong.

Perhaps the ex-husband told them about me.

Damn, damn, damn. Not even a day after the first one, I was caught. Invisible fingers clutched at my brain as I readied to flee. Then the laughter stopped and they all turned to me. The taller copper spoke.

'Ms Pandora Lilly?'

'Yeeesss.' The word struggled from my mouth; by dragging it out long enough, I might delay my inevitable incarceration.

'Ms Pandora Lilly, you do not have to say anything. But,

it may harm your defence if you do not mention when questioned something which you later rely on in court. Anything you do say may be given in evidence. Do you understand this?' I nodded as I reached for the letter opener on my desk. His throat was very inviting. 'Pandora Lilly, I arrest you for the crime of...'

The pause hung in the air as I grabbed the short blade.

Then the silence was shattered by the sound of Stevie Wonder singing *Happy Birthday*. Bob got the streamers out as the coppers removed their uniforms. Someone pushed a chair behind me and I slumped into it as the party kicked off. A glass of champagne was thrust into my hand before I could mutter a single word.

'What?'

The fake police officers were down to their underwear, both of them flirting with Gladys as she stood there openmouthed. Bob sat next to me.

'It's a celebration for you, Pandora.'

'It's not my birthday.' The glass was cold between my fingers.

'I know. It's your six month anniversary since you started here and, well, without you, we'd have gone under by now, so I thought you should get some proper recognition. Most of the workforce, small as it is, don't know what you do here, so it's about time they did.'

I sipped at the drink, with the bubbles tickling the inside of my nose. It smelt of blancmange and tasted of roses.

'Well, thanks, boss, I appreciate it.' I lifted my glass to him, and he returned the gesture.

'You're welcome.'

'Do I get a pay rise as well?'

He laughed and hugged me, my body tensing. When

was the last time someone had touched me that wasn't accompanied by violence? Then, he let go of me with a massive grin on his face and joined the others in the festivities.

That's when I guessed I wouldn't get much work done.

14   JEN: THE BRIDGE

We spent the afternoon making phone calls to social services and getting nowhere. I sent Sutton and Grealish to Betty Green's former workplace, hoping they'd have better luck than Jack and I had. Then we examined the forensic information again in the futile hope something new would jump out as helpful, but it didn't. By the time it hit five o'clock, I'd had enough and could see Jack was itching to leave.

As I went to his desk, I noticed something different about him. While I'd been glued to the computer, he'd sneaked away to have a shave and dowse himself in Giorgio Armani aftershave.

'Have you got a big date planned?'

'Tiffany is taking me to meet her parents.'

I nearly spat my coffee all over his jacket.

'Wow. You'll have a few things in common to talk about, like, you know, growing up watching black and white movies and listening to the Beatles.'

'Ha, ha, Detective Inspector Flowers. You have your fun while you can, but at least I'm dating someone.'

'Being single is not a crime, Jack.'

'If it were, you'd be a career criminal.'

We laughed together, releasing the tension of a frustrating day.

'You know what they say, partner: always stay close to your enemy.'

'I've never known who THEY are. Are they the same people who control the world, getting the rest of us to run around and do their bidding for them?'

'I don't think they're the ones prompting you to chase after a girl half your age, Jack.' I nodded towards his groin. 'We know where that's coming from.'

He placed his arm on my shoulder, transferring his warmth to me and giving my nostrils a precise blast of the aftershave. I felt dizzy and looked forward to cracking open the white wine I'd put in the fridge last night.

'What have you got planned for the evening, Jen? Another exciting night with takeaway food and a bottle of booze, slumped in front of tacky TV shows? So what is it now, *Gogglebox* or a repeat of *Bake Off*?'

He was trying to be funny, but it also felt like he was worried for me.

'Abbey is cooking tonight, a surprise for me, and we'll watch one of her old movies and fight over the popcorn.'

I couldn't think of a better way to relax. As my phone vibrated with a message, I slipped from his grasp and checked the text. He must have noticed my dour expression.

'Is it something serious?'

'No. Abbey's going to Francine's house for band practice. And she'll eat there.'

'So you're all alone again?'

'We're always alone, Jack, even when surrounded by people.'

I don't know why those words slipped out of me, but they did.

'That sounds grim, Jen. Do you want to meet Tiff and me for a meal after we've seen her parents?'

I couldn't think of anything worse. And then I did.

'That's okay, but thanks for the offer.' I removed my phone and checked for what I wanted. 'There are late visiting times at the nursing home, so I'll see my mother.'

I'd need a drink after that, so it was best Abbey wouldn't be around to watch me down a whole bottle of wine in less than an hour. If I added some ice, it could take longer; perhaps I'd make it last for at least two episodes of *The Crown*.

'Are you sure?'

'Of course, partner. You meet your future in-laws, and you can tell me all about it tomorrow.' We smiled together. 'And we might have a break in the case by then.'

We laughed as we left the building and went our separate ways. I thought about what Tiffany's parents would make of him, the man dating their daughter half his age, and tried not to think of the similar situation I was in so long ago.

No, it was wrong to compare those things. I was groomed for two years while my parents stood by and did nothing; Jack's situation was much different. He was the vulnerable one, considering I didn't believe he'd got over his wife kicking him out. But, on the other hand, perhaps he was right, and it was fun for both of them, and it would all blow over soon enough. At least he'd have a better idea after meeting her parents.

I continued to think like that as I drove to see my mother.

WHEN I ARRIVED at the care home, she was in a big room with other residents. There was no live music, but plenty of games were on offer. She was sitting with three others playing cards. The staff member from the last time – her name was Claire – stood next to me.

'What are they playing?' I said.

'Bridge. Do you know the game?'

I did. 'My parents used to play it with a couple from my father's church.' I watched my mother scrutinising her cards, aware she was always very competitive. I moved closer to Claire so no one would hear my words. 'You need a lot of memory retention for Bridge, so won't it be difficult for those with dementia?'

'Yes, it is a challenge for most, but others, like your mother... well, sometimes it can spark their brain into life, especially if they have lots of experience with the game as she has.'

I stood there and observed the group, analysing the changes on her face, recognising the woman from my teenage years. It was as if the last two decades had never happened; unless she had a secret bottle of booze stashed away under the table. The thought of it made my mouth water.

They continued to play as I spoke to Claire.

'The message you left mentioned my mother wanting to tell me something.'

'Yes, yes, she was very excited after your previous visit. I think she wanted to follow you from here until I explained we didn't have your home address.'

'Does she know I'm her daughter?'

'Absolutely. She never stopped mentioning it.' Concern

filled her eyes. 'Was it one of the things she was confused about last time?'

'Yes. That and a few others.'

I watched my mother clap her hands as she and her partner won the latest Bridge rubber.

'What's happening with her fractured ribs?'

'They're healing and she's on strong pain killers. So it's nothing a bit of time won't fix.'

With those words, she went to speak to another resident, and I took a chair opposite the card players. It gave me time to consider what I'd say to my mother; after she told me what was on her mind.

Yes, my mother's mind. She'd never been one to let others know what she was thinking, even, as far as I could tell, her husband. He was a committed Christian, and she showed no interest in religion of any kind. I'd always wondered what they'd seen in each other to end up as a couple, but had never discovered an adequate answer. Perhaps he thought God would grant him a miracle and my mother would convert to his faith.

But not even God could tempt her away from the drink.

Yet, wasn't it the same with my relationships? On reflection, I never understood what I'd seen in those I'd shared my life with – especially the two most important ones: Robert and Ray. I'd tried not to think about either of them over the years, but, as I sat surrounded by people who could barely remember their lives, it seemed appropriate.

Robert was a decision beyond my control. He wormed his way into my life and heart when I was still a child; when I was too young to make rational decisions. Of course, I wasn't the first or the last it would happen to, but I always told myself it had played no significant part in my future.

But how was that possible? Had what happened in

those years between fourteen and sixteen created far-reaching consequences I was still unaware of?

One of those was Ray. I'd married him for stability so Abbey could have a father, so it was no wonder it didn't last long. But, if he'd returned and got in touch, what would I do?

And he must be back if Abbey had seen him at the football match. Was it a coincidence he was there? It seemed unlikely. Which meant he was up to something.

A resident in the far corner took a cigarette from their pocket and lit it. Before the staff could take it from them, the smoke drifted over to me and sent my mind back to the fire-damaged house and the remains of Betty Green.

Was it possible she'd signed off on a report that had removed a child from a family, and then years later, one, or perhaps more, of the parents had returned to take terrible revenge?

The parental bond could be substantial. I knew that because of Abbey, but sometimes I'd let her down or hadn't protected her as I should have. My mother's neglect of me wasn't down to alcohol or dementia; it was in her before those things possessed her. Was it because what she'd told me was right: that I wasn't hers and they'd adopted me after their natural child, their Jenny, was stolen from the hospital? Those things would be easy to discover. A baby abducted from a hospital would have been all over the news, and there were ways for children of adoption to find their birth parents.

But I didn't want to know if her claims were true. It wouldn't excuse her behaviour and would only give me more problems to deal with. Still, it would ease my worries regarding if her dementia was hereditary. Her ailments wouldn't affect Abbey or me if I weren't her blood.

Yet, I was there to answer that question: to see if me imagining my father leaving a message on the answering machine was something I had to worry about. Perhaps I should forget about the whole thing. It hadn't happened again, and maybe Jack was right – it was only a consequence of work-related stress.

So there was no reason for me to sit there, watching someone who had never been a mother to me, regardless of genetics. I observed the glee in her eyes as she continued to win at cards, seeing how much enjoyment she got as she glanced at the others. It was another thing I'd got wrong all these years: her pleasure didn't come from winning, but from others losing.

Whether the baby-snatching story was true or not, she believed it and perhaps had always done so, even before her illness. That was why I was never a daughter to her, why she didn't care about my pregnancy at sixteen to a man more than twice my age.

I left the chair and walked away, not looking at her. My brief family reunion was over and wouldn't happen again. The only problem now was how to explain all of this to Abbey.

Perhaps it was time to tell my daughter the whole truth.

The festivities lasted an hour. I didn't get a pay rise, but I got the tall fake copper's phone number scribbled on the back of a business card. The drinking continued after work, a little gathering in the local pub. And who was I to argue? After all, it was a party for me, and I hadn't experienced one of those for a long time.

Or ever.

I couldn't remember any birthday parties in my past, and every annual celebration – like Christmas or New Year – had always turned into a disaster.

So, even with everything on my mind regarding Betty and what I'd do next, I put it all to the side to enjoy myself.

One of the younger blokes went to the bar and ordered me a drink. It was only just gone six o'clock and I wasn't sure how long the festivities would last. Wary of starting on the double gins too early, I settled on a pint of cider.

We gathered around two tables, eight of us, but more people joined during the night, family and friends of my co-workers. I had none of those to join me, of course. Still, it allowed me to linger on the periphery, keeping my thoughts to myself and focusing on the next person I had to visit. The temptation to go was strong, but I had to fight against it. There was no need to provide the police with two crime scenes to scour in quick succession. The journalist could wait; I knew where he was and I guessed he wouldn't be leaving the city soon. However, I wondered if he'd seen what had happened to the social worker and recognised her name. Perhaps not, since it was so long ago. If he did and he remembered her, would he be worried? I hoped so.

Ten years ago was another world, before new technology revolutionised how we all lived and transformed communication into a mass activity that left many people alone. Then, a sudden image flashed through my head, of the social worker peering at me as the flames rushed up her legs, of seeing the look in her eyes, which wasn't of fear, but more a resigned acceptance of her fate. Maybe she was happy her solitude was ending. Or perhaps it was the realisation her guilt would soon be over.

My mind drifted as people enjoyed themselves around me, my gaze scrutinising the décor of tatty seats, faded wooden tables, and the walls covered with badly drawn caricatures of famous Londoners. A tortured sketch of Queen Victoria stared at me from the opposite wall, with her Majesty surrounded by terrible drawings of David Beckham, Michael Caine, and Helen Mirren. If any of those poor souls were unfortunate enough to stumble into the venue, I'd expect them to sue for defamation of character. Or perhaps it would be deformation.

As I considered how terrible everything was, it got worse with a wall of sound that Phil Spector must have created during a murder spree. A group of poorly designed people jumped from their seats and into the middle of the room, which soon became a makeshift dance floor for those who should have known better, gyrating their hips to a song about refusing to go to rehab. It forced me to down my drink in one and head for another. I ordered more cider as madness disguised as entertainment went on around me.

I didn't return to the table, observing the festivities in full flow from the bar. A DJ in the corner was pretending to spin records while playing a group of digital tracks. He was dressed like The Cat in the Hat with a stripy jumper and large titfer. But my appreciation of his talents increased when he played *Fine Time* by New Order, and then followed it with *Pacific State* by 808 State. I finished the cider and ordered my first gin of the night – it wouldn't be my last – a strawberry and pepper double. By the time the Bee Gees appeared, I was well gone, giddy enough to talk to anyone. The loneliness would return later, I knew that, but I went with the flow.

Everyone seemed to be enjoying the gift of living, yet all I could do was pursue a celebration of death. I knew no other way to live, could think of no alternative to the course I was on. But wasn't life, for most of us, just fleeting glimpses of happiness in between long phases of indifference, depression, and pain? I spent most of my spare time reading, trawling through things I never had access to in school. For several reasons, I struggled through many melancholy periods and tried to find answers to my predicament in religion and philosophy. I quickly discarded the religion, having no patience for that which didn't exist, and became obsessed with philosophical texts.

So I fought with monsters and stared into the abyss, yet still, I found no solutions. But I had a reason to live and could bear most any pain now.

All apart from one.

No matter how much I drank, how much I covered myself with other people's joy, that pain would never leave me. And I knew it wouldn't, even when I completed my mission. There was no escaping from it, just like there was no escaping for those who gave me this pain. The social worker was the first, but not the last.

The DJ reached into the 1960s and played *Light My Fire* by The Doors. I nearly spat my gin over the tattooed bloke standing next to me at the bar. What a waste that would have been. I listened to the music and perceived it as a sign from above; me, a dedicated atheist. For that moment, through the haze of sweat, alcohol, and belief that all dreams could come true, I believed a Greater Power was guiding me to complete my quest. Not that I needed an extra push.

I clutched my glass and dodged the swaying drunks on the dance floor, or perhaps they avoided me, and went to the DJ. I shot him my best enigmatic smile and he moved forward.

'Have you got a request, love?'

I certainly had. I told him what I wanted and he nodded in acquiescence. By the time I returned to the bar for my next drink, the first bars of the greatest ever song were floating towards me.

Don't fear the reaper, they sang.

Don't fear the reaper.

WHEN I ARRIVED HOME, I ordered a pizza and opened a bottle of wine. The fake copper's phone number lay on the kitchen table.

When was the last time I'd gone on a date? Darren didn't count, of course.

This was the third part of my life, and I was sure the last proper date must have been towards the tail end of the first part. What was his name? My memory of it was hazy, just fading images of a man who looked like Elvis and smelt of fish. I could have forgiven that if he'd resembled the early Elvis, with the slicked-back quiff and orgasm-inducing hips, and not the bloke who died on the toilet with a burger in his hands.

I pushed the image from my head and picked up the paper, going over the phone number several times until it cemented itself at the front of my brain. Perhaps he didn't want a date and was only after sex – a one-night stand. I wasn't opposed to that. It might bring a slither of joy into my life, no matter how fleeting.

I finished the drink and poured another, remembering how he moved in the office, picturing his impressive half-naked torso and a smile that glittered like gold. The image played on a loop as I drank half the bottle of wine, thankful the pizza turned up before I got too merry. I chewed on ham and cheese while planning what to say to him on the phone.

But it would wait until tomorrow.

I grabbed the last of the booze and the food to retire to the other room. Then I switched on the laptop and bit on a chunk of ice. The rest of the night was spent searching for information on the social worker's death. I didn't like to call it murder. Justice wasn't murder.

Most of what I found were reports stating how the police had no clues to the crime and that their investigation was ongoing. There were a few posts on websites in memoriam for the social worker, but I felt nothing for those.

Green had kept a terrible secret and had paid the price for that. I had no guilt, no remorse.

By the time I finished the second bottle of wine, I felt little of anything.

16 JEN: THE PSYCHOLOGIST

I slept through the alarm on Tuesday morning. It had been a restless night, with my mind full of burnt bodies and my mother's face. I wasn't sure which was worse. By the time I was dressed and downstairs, Abbey had left. There was a note on the table from her.

I've got football practice after school. Can you pick me up at six?

The thump in my head increased as I poured myself a cup of coffee and texted her a confirmation. Then I retreated to the living room and stared at the time – nine o'clock. I should have been at work an hour ago. Before I could ready an excuse, the phone rang. I considered ignoring it, but understood my partner would be persistent.

'I'm sorry, Jack. I'll be there soon.' My voice sounded as if broken glass covered my tongue.

'You should take the day off, Jen. I know you had a bad night.'

'Are you a mind reader?'

'Abbey texted me this morning. Said you had nightmares.'

'Did I?'

The memories weren't great, but I wouldn't have called them nightmares. Yet, why did I feel terrible now, as if my head was underwater in a microwave?

'I'm okay. I can't let you do all the work on this case.'

'There's nothing much to do, Jen. The only leads we have are Darren Green's mysterious date and social services. And both are flimsy.'

He wasn't wrong.

'That's why we need to talk to people who worked with Betty Green.'

'If any of them are still there after ten years. And I can take Constable Sutton with me. Grealish is speaking to the neighbours, so we have everything covered.'

'Thanks. You know how to make a girl feel wanted.'

'It's not that, Jen. You haven't had a break in a while, and we don't want you...'

He didn't finish the sentence, so I did it for him.

'You don't want me hallucinating again.'

'We don't know that's what happened with your father's message. Did you see your mother yesterday?'

'I saw her, but we didn't talk. So I won't be going back. I'm leaving my past alone.'

'And Abbey?'

'I'll tell her everything.'

That was a lie. There would be no mention of what happened to me at sixteen.

'Maybe you should talk to someone, Jen.'

'I'm talking to you, Jack.'

'A professional. It can't hurt.'

I was impressed with his advice, considering he'd bottled up all of his emotions since the separation from his wife and kids.

'I'll think about it. Keep me informed about how the case is going.'

'Will do. And take care of yourself.'

I put the phone down and finished my drink. Then I left the house and drove out of London.

AN HOUR LATER, I was sitting in the office of Doctor Felicia Nelson drinking more coffee, knowing I'd need the toilet soon. It was that time between breakfast and lunch, and I still hadn't eaten. There was a pain in my stomach, but it wasn't from hunger.

'Are you sure you want nothing to eat, Jen? I can make you a healthy smoothie. It's no trouble.'

She cradled a large ginger cat in her lap, its saucer-like eyes burrowing deep into me.

'No, I'm fine, Felicia.'

I'd met her last year and she'd helped Abbey through a difficult time.

The moggy purred as she stroked it. 'How have you been? It's been a while since we've spoken.'

'I'm fine.' Another lie for the day. 'I needed to get out of London for a while.'

Which wasn't untrue.

'Is Abbey okay?'

'She's great, Doc. She has her own band now and is the star player in the school football team. She still says good things about you.'

The cat jumped from her lap. 'I'm glad I was of some help.' She reached down by the side of her chair and got a bottle of water. After a quick swig, she scrutinised me. 'Is this a professional call?'

I hesitated with a reply, considering how much to tell her. Yet, what was the point of going all the way there to hold back on the truth?

'I think I might be losing my mind, Felicia.'

She put the bottle on the floor. 'Start from the beginning, Jen.'

So I did. From the phone message I believed I'd got from my father to my recent encounters with my mother.

'When did you receive this message?' She spoke as if it had happened.

'Three months ago.'

'And there have been no others since?'

'Not that I can remember.'

'Abbey didn't hear it?'

'No, she didn't. I deleted it straight away.' At least, I think I did.

'What was happening in your life at the time?'

'Oh, the usual: a murder case and my daughter starting a rock band. Nothing out of the ordinary.'

'And your sleep and eating patterns?'

'Little of the first and plenty of junk for the second.'

'Alcohol intake?'

'Always.'

'Has it increased?'

'A bit.'

Felicia rested her arms on her legs.

'There are many reasons people hallucinate, Jen.'

'I bet none of them is good.'

'Drug-induced hallucinations are visual, but they may affect other senses. They can include flashes of light, abstract shapes or take the form of an animal or person. More often, visual distortions alter the person's perception of the world around them. Well, yours was visual and auditory. You saw the light flashing on the machine and heard the voice. People can experience hallucinations when high on illegal drugs such as amphetamines, cocaine, LSD, or ecstasy. They can also occur during withdrawal from alcohol or drugs if you suddenly stop taking them.

'The hallucinations can happen on their own or as a part of drug-induced psychosis. After long-term drug use, they may cause schizophrenia. Heavy alcohol use can also lead to psychotic states, hallucinations and dementia.'

'I promise you, Felicia; there were no drugs involved. Booze, yes, but nothing else.'

'If you add that to your lack of sleep, poor diet, and stress from an extended workload, it would explain your hallucination, if it was one. Those factors I mentioned, are they still relevant?'

'Well, I'm off work now, and Abbey's happier than I've ever seen her.'

'But she's asking questions about your past, hers and yours, plus there's your mother.'

'Do you think her dementia is hereditary?'

'It's possible, but unlikely. I can arrange for you to have a CT scan of the brain if it concerns you?'

'No, that's okay.' It was the last thing I needed to confirm.

'Then my advice is to cut your work hours, include more fruit and veg in your diet, drink lots of water, reduce your alcohol intake and maybe get a bit of exercise. And enjoy your time with your daughter. If you feel you have another hallucination, call me straight away.'

She told me most of what I already knew, but it was good to have confirmation. I stood to leave and offered my hand.

'Thank you, Felicia. I feel better now.'

'No problem, Jen.' A different cat entered the room and rubbed at her legs. 'What will you do about your mother's claims?'

'The adoption?' I'll ignore them.

'I'm sure you already know, but you can check her story.'

I finished shaking her hand. 'I'll think about it.'

I left her house and thought about it for thirty seconds.

Then I drove to the nearest coffee shop for a drink and something to eat. The ham and cheese toasty crunched through my teeth and down into my stomach as I searched the internet. Typing "baby snatched from hospital" into Google produced 2,630,000 results from all over the world. Before narrowing it down to the UK, I scanned some results, reading the stories of those abducted and found again, sometimes decades later. There was even one of a teenage girl called Abbie. It sent a shiver down my spine, but I read it anyway.

In July 1994, baby Abbie Humphries was snatched from the hospital at just three hours old and kept captive for seventeen days. Her parents, Karen and Roger, didn't know if their daughter was alive or dead. The crime caused a sensation, with Princess Diana sending a goodwill message to the distraught family as they waited for news.

The police tracked down the disturbed woman who had taken the baby, and there was a quote from Abbie when she was seventeen about the abduction.

I learned how hard the police worked looking for me — perhaps that's why I've been thinking about joining up. Maybe I'll end up as a detective.

The coincidences in the report sent a shiver down my spine, and I browsed through other stories of snatched babies from hospitals. There were more than I expected, but mine happened thirty-seven years ago, if it was true. How likely was that to be online?

I added the year and the UK as keywords to the search. There were 855,000 results, but one stood out from the others – a baby girl who went missing for seventeen days after a woman posing as a health visitor took her from London's St Thomas's hospital.

It wasn't the coincidence that the baby was missing for seventeen days like Abbie Humphries that sparked my interest, but the report stating the girl was the first baby kidnapped from a UK maternity ward. This was in 1990, five years after I was born. So my mother's story was untrue if that was the first child abduction from a maternity ward.

I relaxed into the chair and reached for the large cream cake I'd bought. Jam dripped from the side, the stories of abducted babies shrinking from my mind. Part of me was disappointed and I didn't know why. Bits of cake crumbled in my mouth before I understood my feelings: if I was adopted, then it meant those I'd always believed were my parents weren't. Not that I thought I'd start a search for my birth parents, but at least I could confirm I wasn't related by blood to those who'd raised me. I was pondering these thoughts when I received a text from Jack.

No luck at social services. Only two are still there who worked with Betty Green, and they said she always kept to herself. The manager claimed they don't keep records of verbal or written threats to staff, but said they are pretty regular. I'm heading back to work to type this up. There's no need for you to come in. See how you feel tomorrow.

I replied my thanks, put the phone away, and finished the coffee.

My mother's claims were untrue, my hallucination was likely from stress and overwork, and Abbey was doing great.

However, I needed to tell her a few things. I was sure we'd catch a lead in the Betty Green murder soon enough. A killer with that much anger towards Green wouldn't be able to sleep easily. Guilt would eat them up at every minute of the day.

As the song said, things could only get better.

I turned from the mirror, facing the man I'd come to see, aware that I kept my real face in a box deep inside my head but always ready to show to the world.

James Cole peered at a piece of paper on his desk.

'How did you find me, Ms Brooks?'

I removed the scarf from my neck, exposing the scar along the top of my shoulder, watching him trying not to stare at it. It was strange how something painful from such a long time ago could help me now. I moved forward an inch and he switched his gaze from the wound, peering through the window of his third-floor office. He was distracted enough not to notice me removing the knife from my bag.

'Someone in the pub mentioned your name, and then I found your website.'

He pulled at the top of his shirt as he turned to me. He was nervous about something. Did he know who I was? The small blade hidden in my clenched hand cut into my skin. I stopped the blood dripping on the floor by wiping my fingers along my leg. Leaving evidence of my DNA in the room would be fatal.

Cole's attempted smile crawled over his lips.

'Which pub was that, Ms Brooks?'

'The Wheatsheaf in Camden. Do you know it?'

He pretended to look at his computer screen and shook his head. 'Can't say I do.'

I beamed at him. 'Still, your website is curious.'

He returned his gaze to me. 'In what way?'

My laugh made my eyebrows flutter. 'Well, no offence, Mr Cole, but it looks like a twelve-year-old trapped in the 1990s designed it.'

I expected him to scowl, but he only laughed. 'You're not far wrong. I'm terrible with computers, apart from typing and email, so I got my nephew to create it. He's sixteen and never leaves his room; it's sad.' He opened the top drawer of his desk and removed a packet of gum. He slipped a piece into his mouth without offering me any. 'If you think the website is amateurish, why did you contact me?'

The sudden smell of fake strawberries didn't hide the sneer in his voice. I flapped my eyelashes at him and smiled.

'Oh, don't get me wrong, I think it's charming. I couldn't wait to meet you after seeing that.'

He continued to chew as he spoke. 'So, what can I do for you, Ms Brooks?'

I fluttered some more and pushed my hands towards him, the pink of my nails contrasting with the darkness in his eyes.

'I need you to find my daughter.'

He swallowed the gum and pressed two fingers against his chest.

'Missing persons is my speciality, so you've come to the right place.'

I pulled my chair closer to the desk. 'Please, call me Louise.'

My smile was so bright, I felt it warming my cheeks. Would he recognise that name, be intrigued by it and ask me about it?

No. Cole leant into the computer, his harsh fingers tapping on the keyboard as he entered the details I'd provided, all of them as fake as my name. It took him ten minutes before he asked me the question I'd been waiting for.

'Do you have a photograph of Libby?'

The knife was under my leg, pressed between my trousers and the chair, leaving my hand free to reach down for the bag and the photo inside. I removed it, holding it close to my palm, fighting not to let the emotions defeat me. It was the same image the media had published, the same one I knew he'd seen before. I placed it on the desk and pushed it towards him, waiting for the private investigator to recognise it and remember.

But he only glanced at it, fixated on the computer screen. Then, he grabbed more gum and threw it into his mouth as he typed. The movement of his lips; the way he chewed; the rhythm of his jaw matching that of his fingers on the keyboard: all of it increased the heat flowing through me.

My head felt like a leaky microwave as I cleared my throat.

'How long have you been a private investigator, Mr Cole?'

I dug a nail into my wrist and left it there, not cutting the skin. He didn't lift his face from the computer, but he'd stopped typing.

'About five years.'

I think he was already bored and was probably staring at something on the internet. If I grabbed the screen from him, what would I see? BBC sport, some music video with the sound down, online gambling, his social media page, or perhaps a porn site?

'You were a journalist before this?'

That stopped him in his tracks. Cole's fingers hovered over the keyboard as he lifted his head to me, the shadows around his eyes growing by the second. His voice popped like a broken radio transmission as he spoke.

'That was a long time ago.'

'Ten years, wasn't it, when you worked for one of the local papers? I remember your columns. You were a crime reporter, right?'

He focused on me for the first time since I'd entered his office, scrutinising me under a giant microscope, both hands placed on the desk.

'Do I know you, Ms Brooks?'

His hand was close to the photo, but it may as well have been on another planet.

'No, Mr Cole, we've never met. But you know her.'

I nodded at the image. Then, as he twisted his head to look at it, I pounced forward with the blade, plunging it through his palm so hard, it embedded itself into the wood. His scream was loud, and I was glad the rest of the building was empty. As he used his free hand to grasp at the knife, I delved into my bag and removed the bottle of petrol. I sprayed it over him as he struggled to free his hand. Finally, I placed the container on the desk and lit a match. He glared at me.

'Are you fucking mad?'

'Sit down, or I'll set you on fire, Jim.'

The flame flickered in my fingers. All it would take was

one flick to set him alight. But not yet. Agony and anger crisscrossed his face in thick lines as he sat while avoiding more damage to his hand. The office smelt of sweat and gasoline as he struggled to speak.

'What do you want?'

'Good, Jim, cut to the chase. There's no point spending longer here than necessary.' I blew the flame out before it kissed my flesh. I dropped the match into my pocket and retrieved the photograph. 'Are you still going to pretend not to recognise her?'

His chest rose and fell like an asthmatic lift. 'I never knew who she was.'

'But you know what happened to her.'

Sweat gushed down his face and collected in the dimple in his chin.

'No, no, I don't. She disappeared; that's all I know. This was ten years ago.'

'She wasn't the only child who vanished, was she? And you were investigating them for the newspaper.'

'Kids disappear all the time, especially in London. It was a dead-end, so my editor forced me to stop.'

I removed another match.

'That's not what I heard, Jim. You told your employer you were retiring as a journalist and quit. Then you had three years doing nothing, but still with enough finances to continue living in that nice flat of yours and going abroad on holiday at least twice a year. And then you started this business.' I glanced around the room, staring at the damp on the walls. 'I guess you'd spent most of your payoff, so this was the best you could do.'

The aroma of fresh blood joined the stink of petrol as it dribbled down his imprisoned hand.

'Payoff?'

I rolled the match between my fingers.

'Don't deny it, Jim. Someone paid you to kill your story about the missing kids and look the other way, didn't they?'

His breathing had returned to normal, his gaze fixed on me.

'I don't know what you're talking about.'

I saw the machinations unfurling behind his eyes, wondering how long he'd wait before ignoring the pain in his hand and lunging for me. I moved closer to the desk to tempt him. But not before he told me what I needed.

'The social worker gave me your name, Jim; you know, the one who provided you with the details for the missing kids during your investigation. She claimed not to know who was behind the abductions, but, just like you, she lived well beyond her means the last ten years. Her lies didn't do her any good.'

'Was it you who killed her, who set her on fire?'

I grinned at him. 'I can see why you're a private investigator, Jim.' I leant over the desk and reduced the gap between us. 'The only thing you need to ask yourself now is if you want to remain a live one.'

He grabbed at me with his free hand, but his reflexes were slow, and I dodged his lunge by stepping back. I'd expected it, but the next bit took me by surprise. Cole ripped his palm from the wood, taking splinters and the knife with him. Flesh and blood dripped on the desk as he grinned at me.

'You should have lit that match when you could, girl.'

My spine kissed the wall as I laughed. 'Is that the best insult you can do?' I shook my head. 'I haven't been a girl in a long time.' The laughter left me just as quickly as it had come. 'But my daughter was still a girl when she disappeared, and I think you know where she is.'

Cole removed the blade and stepped around the desk.

'When the police get here, I'll tell them you attacked me and what I did was in self-defence.' He used his good hand to wipe the sweat from his lips. 'Which is true.'

'You could let me leave, Jim.'

He shook his head. 'No, I don't think so. Whatever craziness is possessing you isn't going to go away. You'll return and attack me again, I guarantee it. I need to end this now.'

I arched my back into the wall. 'Or you could just tell me what I want to know.'

'Was she your daughter?'

Speaking of her in the past tense sent daggers into my heart. I ignored his question with one of my own.

'Who are you covering up for?'

He waved the knife at me, his anger abated.

'You're off your head, lady. Get out of here before I change my mind.'

My bag was near the desk, on the floor between us. I pointed at it.

'I'll need that. My purse and money are in there.'

Cole aimed the blade at me. 'Not before I check it first. You might have another knife in there.'

He turned from me and moved for the bag. I could have left then, slipped out the door and forgotten about him. But that was never an option. Instead, I stepped forward and kicked him in the back of the leg. He fell, banging his head on the chair and dropping the blade. I pushed it away with my foot and scooped up my bag. The matches were in my fingers as he struggled to his feet.

'Tell me who paid you off or suffer the consequences.'

I removed a match and lit it.

Cole leant into the front of the desk, dripping blood as a

giant purple bruise formed on his forehead. The intensity in my eyes must have convinced him of my intentions.

'The copper threatened me, said he'd kill my parents if I didn't give him everything I had. So I did. And then I got a lump sum of cash.'

'The copper?'

'Yes, from the Met.'

This was unexpected news. Were the police involved?

'So you kept quiet and ran away.'

'What else could I do?'

'Give me his name and I'll let you live.'

So he did, but I didn't. I was on the street by the time he stopped screaming.

Andy Greenham and his team from the Fire and Rescue Services had controlled the situation when Jack and I arrived. We stood outside the building in Brixton, dressed in our protective gear and waiting for the all-clear to go inside. I sidled up to my partner.

'I was about to head home and sit down with Abbey for a curry when I got the call.'

'You can cook now?'

Athena Temple came out the door as I stopped myself from cuffing him around the ear. I wasn't lying about the food, and my stomach grumbled to remind me it was seven hours since I'd eaten. She must have heard the noise rumbling out of me.

'It's not as bad as the previous scene, DI Flowers, but if you're going to throw up, take a bag with you.'

I forced a smile at her. 'What did you find upstairs, Athena?'

'One body, male, not as badly burned as the last victim, probably because they put up a fight. There's something interesting on the desk, though.'

'Which is?'

'Best if you two see it first-hand.'

Fire Investigation Officer Greenham signalled us to follow him into the building and upstairs.

'The blaze was even more contained here, in the office. It's on the third floor.'

I stepped behind him. 'Do we know who the victim is?'

'There are enough teeth left to make an ID, but James Cole owns the business.'

'What type of business?' Jack said.

Greenham turned to me. 'Private investigations.'

I prevented myself from humming the Dire Straits tune and thought about the places we passed on the way up.

'There were no witnesses in the other offices?'

'All of them have been shut for at least six months. Cole's was the only one still open.'

We were outside the door imprinted with the name Cole Investigation Services. The smell of fire wasn't strong; it was so subtle I thought we might be in the wrong place. However, I soon discounted that idea when we walked inside, seeing the blackened body behind the desk and the lingering haze of smoke hanging over everything. And that stink of smelling burnt human flesh.

Athena had been right: the destruction wasn't as fierce as at Betty Green's house. None of the walls was damaged, and the floor seemed clear until I strode around the desk and saw the damage to the floorboards.

'He was standing behind the desk when set alight.' Greenham nodded at Cole's remains. 'The fire would have been intense, but he must have fallen back.' He pointed at the ash and burn marks on the wall. 'Then it looks like he fell forward over the desk, where he still had the strength to grab the pen and write that into the wood.'

I went closer to the front of the desk, peering at the pen melted between his fingers; and the one word he'd written.

PAIN

'It must have been excruciating,' Jack said.

I moved towards the window, gazing down at the police cars and crowd gathering on the street. Then I returned to Greenham.

'There's a lot of wood in here – why didn't more of it go up in flames?'

He stepped near to me. 'I wasn't sure at the Green house, but I think the same thing happened there and here.'

'Which is what?'

'Whoever did this ensured the fire wouldn't spread beyond the victim.'

Jack peered at the writing in the wood. 'How would they do that?'

Greenham pointed at the open door of the office. 'There's a kitchen and sink through there. I checked it before you arrived. Perhaps the killer used it to bring water through to contain the blaze once they knew Cole couldn't survive.'

'And they did the same at Betty Green's house?'

He nodded. 'It's a working theory.'

I walked into the corridor and entered the room opposite. There was an empty Pot Noodle in the bin and a washbasin in the sink, as well as a few plates and a kettle. I pictured the scene in my head, producing a terrible image of Cole doused in petrol, and then set alight. Then he struggled against the flames, falling back, and then forward before, in desperation, grabbing the pen. Finally, I visualised our killer standing there, observing, watching the fruits of their handiwork, ensuring Cole would die before going to get water to control the fire.

Jack stepped near me. 'Why not just let the whole office go up in flames and the building? That would destroy the crime scene and any evidence left behind.'

I turned to him. 'They don't want anyone else to get hurt, same as at Green's house.'

'We have a killer who's concerned about others?' Jack said.

I pointed at the sink. 'We need to check everything for fingerprints and do the same in Betty Green's kitchen.'

We exited the building, stepping into the night and removing the protective uniforms. The wind swept across my face, sending a chill through my bones. A street food van was frying chicken somewhere nearby and my stomach rumbled again. I hoped Abbey had left me some of the takeaway.

'Do you think this is the same murderer?' Jack said.

I shrugged. 'Two murders in three days where the victim was burnt alive? If it's not the same person, that's some coincidence.'

'But why here?' He looked up at the window on the third floor. 'What connects a private investigator with a retired social worker?'

That was the sixty-four thousand dollar question.

'We need to dig into James Cole's life; there must be a connection between him and Betty Green.' My guts rumbled.

Jack shook his head. 'Do you want something to eat? You know you can't work on an empty stomach.'

It was tempting. If I were out of the house and in a restaurant, I wouldn't feel guilty about drinking. And we could talk about the case. But I didn't want to leave Abbey at home again. Not that she needed to have me around; it was more about me needing to be near her. You could never wash the scenes of violence from your head. Even the alcohol couldn't do that, but being around everyday ordinary domesticity would be nice for a change. That's if I could find it at our house.

'You should spend some time with Tiffany, Jack.' I strode towards my car. 'It's never too early to get the wedding invitations organised.'

The scowl on his face made his eyes appear darker than they were.

'Ha bloody ha, Jennifer.'

I must have hit a raw nerve. Or I was closer to the truth than my joke intended.

'Still, there won't be many from your side, will there?'

He watched me open the car door. 'You're only jealous.'

I put my hand on his shoulder. 'I'm happy for you, partner, but I need to get back and see Abbey, or she'll think I don't exist.'

'I know, Jen. I hardly get time with the boys nowadays. If they weren't part of that football team, I wouldn't see them at all. If I didn't have work to focus on, I'd lose my mind.'

He appeared to have accepted there would be no reconnection with his wife, but it had been clear for a while how much he missed his sons, Tom and Jack Junior. Seeing the pain in his eyes only made me want to go home even more.

I slipped my hand from him. 'Once we get this case solved, we can organise something together with the kids.'

About two years ago, Abbey had had a crush on Tom, but I'd nipped that in the bud. Perhaps it might be good for her now to talk to boys, and it would be easier if it were one of Jack's kids. Easier for me to control.

Jack nodded at me. 'That sounds great, partner. Let's

hope we can link Green and Cole together sooner rather than later.'

With that, we got into our cars and drove away. A low wail moaned at me from my guts all the way home, and I prayed Abbey hadn't eaten all the Indian food.

Voices were coming from the living room when I stepped inside. I dumped my jacket behind the door and walked into the room, expecting to see Francine with Abbey; instead, I got the shock of my life and hoped I was hallucinating again.

Abbey jumped off the sofa. 'Mum, look who's here.'

It was impossible not to look at the man sitting in my house: my ex-husband, Ray Simpson. My mouth must have been hanging open as wide as it could get since a draught raced down my throat. He stood and offered me his hand as if he was at a job interview.

'Hello, Jen. Long time, no see.'

That was the understatement of the century. I took his hand, grasping it for a second before letting go, too worried if I held on for long, the past would come rushing back into my life and I'd discover the last twelve years had been nothing but an illusion.

Or perhaps a hallucination.

Before I could reply, Abbey spoke.

'Ray was at football practice tonight and we got talking, and I knew you'd ordered a takeaway, so I thought I'd invite him. I knew you wouldn't mind.'

There was just a hint of desperation in her voice as I stared at him.

'You were at Abbey's football practice?'

'I should have told you, Mum. Ray's been there all week.'

Cold fingers slithered inside me and gripped at my heart as I scrutinised my ex-husband.

'I thought you were living abroad, Ray.'

'That's right, Jen, I was.' He glanced between Abbey and me as if there was a secret she knew, but I didn't. I'd seen the same look many times before in interview rooms when one criminal was contemplating ratting another one out. 'But something important arose, so I came home.'

'To see Abbey and me?'

'It's important.'

'I'll get some drinks,' Abbey said before dashing out to the kitchen. He smiled at her as she left.

'I told Abbey the news earlier. I'd wanted to see you first, but you're a hard woman to pin down.'

'That's what working for the Met does to you, Ray.'

'You've come a long way since we were together, Jen.' He glanced around the room. 'A bigger house and a promotion: Detective Inspector now.'

My irritation amplified my hunger and desire for a stiff drink.

'Tell me why you're here, Ray.'

'I think you'd better sit down, Jen.'

The heat increased inside my veins. 'After all this time, you're still telling me what to do.'

He shook his head. 'I didn't come all this way for a fight.'

Abbey was taking a long time to return with the drinks.

'Just tell me then.' I didn't sit down.

He took a deep breath. 'I've got less than a month to live, Jen. I need to inform everyone I know.'

I allowed my legs to buckle and flopped onto the sofa behind me. As I hit it, Abbey returned and handed me a cold bottle of Mexican lager. She looked me in the eye as I downed half of it before she slumped next to me. Then we stared at him together.

I didn't know what to say. We were close once, but not that close. We were under no illusions it was love and both knew it wouldn't last. It was an amicable enough divorce, yet we'd never stayed in touch.

So I wanted to ask him why, when he had so little time left, did he want to see people he'd stopped caring about more than a decade ago? But of course, I couldn't say that; it would have been harsh and cruel. So I said the only thing any decent human would do in the situation.

'I'm so sorry, Ray.'

All he did was shrug. '*C'est la vie*. My time is just about up, so I need to make amends.'

'There's nothing to make amends for, Ray.'

'Well, I could have been a better husband to you and a proper father to Abbey, but there's no point dwelling on that now.' He reached into his pocket and handed me a piece of paper. 'I've done okay since we split, Jen.' I thought that might be a little dig at me until I saw the sincerity on his face. 'And I'd like to leave something for Abbey's future.'

I scanned the paper, but the fuzz in my head meant the words were just like alphabet soup in a blender.

'What is this, Ray?'

'I've deposited it into a trust fund until she's eighteen and given you Power of Attorney over it until she's twenty-one.'

The words and numbers all blurred into one until Abbey snatched it from me.

'Fuck!'

I should have told her off for swearing, but I knew how

she felt. Then, before I could say anything, my dying ex-husband spoke again.

'Is that Indian food I smell in the kitchen?' He rubbed at his belly. 'I haven't had a decent curry in ages.'

Mexican lager slipped into the pit of my stomach as numbers swirled around inside my head.

19 PANDORA: THE REBIRTH

Gin covered my shirt as I lay on the kitchen floor, staring at the damp on the ceiling. In the far corner were some words I'd always assumed one of the previous tenants had somehow scrawled there. I pushed my elbows into the cold tiles and strained my eyesight to see what was written above me, struggling to make it out, but getting there.

You can never lose what you don't have.

How true that was.

I rolled on my side and watched a cockroach drown in the tonic I'd spilt earlier. Perhaps I was witnessing my future, my reincarnation as an insect because of the terrible things I'd done by killing those people. Regret and guilt were old friends of mine, and I'd expected a tinge of those twin lovers to visit me once I started on this journey, but I believed the obvious guilt of my victims would spare me such vicissitudes. Yet, in the middle of the night, the pain had come roaring back and reignited the depression I'd spent so much time trying to bury deep inside me.

The darkness threatened to engulf me until I used my

surroundings to fight it off. How old was this flat and how many people had lived here before me? From the outside, the block looked like it had been built in the 1960s. One of those places architects and town planners thought was the future but only resembled the concrete styles borrowed from the Soviet Bloc: tall, imposing, devoid of character, and utilitarian. Yet, in some respects, it reminded me of me.

I wondered if any of the previous tenants from the last sixty years had been like me, solitary and alone, or perhaps it had housed happy families, joyful kids, and fulfilled parents. But how many times had the walls peered down at residents who were struggling not to sink below their own despair?

My legs buckled as I stood. Everything was placed on the table from earlier: the bottles of gin I'd bought from Aldi; the painkillers stockpiled over the months from various shops; the petrol in its shiny container; the lighter and a box of matches in case the lighter didn't work. I knew the guilt would come at some point – I may be a murderer, but I'm not heartless – but not before I'd completed my tasks. Yet when it came, I could do nothing about it apart from drinking and organising the items on the table as a panacea.

But it was a remedy I didn't want to administer, not yet.

I glanced around the room, staring at the place I'd never shared with anyone, peering at the chairs only for me and the plates which were only ever used for one. It shouldn't be like that, of course. Humans were not designed to be solitary beings; it's not in our DNA. On the contrary, we require company and conversation; we desire to be touched and held, to be loved and to love.

And I'd lost my opportunity for that. Or, more accurately, I'd had it taken from me, snatched away when I couldn't do anything about it.

But I could do something now.

I stared at the instruments of death on the table and wondered how brave I'd be when it was my life to be ended.

I AWOKE SOMETIME LATER, unsure of how much time had passed. A red light flashed on my phone across from me on the floor. Had I tried to call someone? Or maybe it was work wondering where I was. To my surprise, I'd grown fond of some people there in the last few days. The party had instigated those feelings, showing how my colleagues – none of whom I was close to – looked upon me so kindly. Perhaps I could use those burgeoning relationships and friendships to fill the void in my life. It was a comforting thought, but I wasn't convinced.

My body was twisted out of shape on the tiles. I appeared to have lost half my clothes while I was unconscious, and my naked legs stuck to the floor as I curled into the foetal position. It was a warm feeling which flowed through me, as if I was returning to the beginning, to how I'd started, and now I could reset my life.

A sharp pain screamed through my guts and I turned on my side to retch, a wretched creature giving back their bile to the world. Another cockroach scampered towards me from underneath the cooker, running so fast on its many legs, I thought it was related to the one who'd died earlier, and now it was hurtling for its revenge.

But revenge isn't sweet – it's sickly and painful and brings no great reward. At first, you revel in it, grasping the rush of pleasure it delivers. But, if you have empathy, which

I do, it clutches at your heart and tries to tear out everything which makes you human.

It was comforting, lying there like that, a return to the womb, fighting to regain that part of my life before it all went wrong. So I pulled into myself, ignoring the stink of my vomit and the sweat under my armpits. What lay on the table wasn't for me, not now; there were others I needed to warm up first before I got the answers I sought. Then, and only then, could I consider what my future would be.

I couldn't plan for the future until the past was dealt with.

20   JEN: THE PUB

'Jesus Christ, Jen, how did you handle that?'

We were standing outside The Wheatsheaf at nine in the morning and I'd just told Jack about my meeting with my ex-husband. The place stank of last night's beer and stale piss. I nursed the cup of coffee in my hand, letting its warmth wash through me and using its aroma to push back the other smells lingering inside my head.

'Which part? Ray telling me he's dying or that he's leaving Abbey a hundred grand in his will?'

As he considered my words, I twisted my neck to stare around this part of Camden. We were here to meet someone James Cole had employed as a so-called surveillance expert for his private investigation business. But being here had stirred up some memories of my formative years frequenting the Camden nightlife. Or perhaps it was because of Ray's visit.

We'd passed the Roundhouse on the way, the venue of my favourite gig. Just seeing the building as I drove past it had resurrected images of that night: of me squashed into the crowd and forcing myself down to the front. It had been my last year at university. I was twenty-one and fewer than six months away from giving birth to Abbey. I'd missed the Zutons and ignored the Sugababes as support, too busy knocking back tequila shots in the bar, preparing myself for the main event.

I've since realised that James Brown was tiny, like Prince, but he seemed like a giant on that night. I had a vague memory of the actor Max Beesley being on stage, but the sounds in my mind were all the Godfather of Soul: *Funky Good Time*, *Soul Man*, *I Feel Good*, and *It's A Man's Man's Man's World*. A gospel choir joined him at the end and, as Jack stared at me now, I still heard their heavenly sounds.

'The dying bit, not the money. How is Abbey doing with the news?'

'She appears unfazed, but it's hard for me to get a read on her nowadays. If she's not there when I get home, she's either with Francine in the band or with the football team. I was worried she might have taken on too much, but at least she'll be busy enough not to think about Ray's health.'

Or obsess about what she'd do with the money.

The pub was already open, one of those places that serves breakfasts from eight in the morning. But we were waiting to go inside; our appointment wasn't due for another fifteen minutes.

'It must have been a shock for you, seeing him in the house when you got home.'

'My whole life is one long shock at the moment, Jack.'

'Is that it, then, or will you see Ray again?'

Two pensioners strode past us and entered the pub. They smelt of woodbines and whisky, and I realised I was thinking of my mother again.

'He's going to Scotland today to visit some of his old friends. So I told him to get in touch when he returned.'

Jack's guts grumbled. 'Okay.' He rubbed at his stomach. 'Can we go in now? I haven't eaten since yesterday.'

I finished the coffee and dropped the cup into a bin. 'Sure, why not?'

He didn't need a second invitation, pushing his way in and heading for the bar while I found a table near the window. I didn't know what the guy we were meeting looked like, but according to Constable Sutton, who'd set it up, this Mike Ryan would recognise us.

'I ordered you a bacon sandwich.' Jack sat next to me. 'Did you read the message Sutton sent this morning?'

I narrowed my eyes at him. 'How else would I be here?'

'You know what I mean. She included details regarding the cash Cole had lost last year and how his business was on the verge of bankruptcy.'

He glanced at the bar as if the food would arrive a minute after he'd paid for it.

'You think someone killed him because he owed them money?'

'No, of course not. But it shows how worried he must have been. And when that happens, people do desperate things.'

The smell of alcohol lingering in the room tickled at my insides.

'I think it's more likely it's connected to a client of his or an ex-client.' I stretched out my legs, resisting the temptation to kick off my shoes. 'After Ray left last night, I checked Cole's PI website. It looked like it was from twenty years ago, but it seems his main line of work was Matrimonial Investigation.'

Jack tapped one finger on the table like a drug addict going cold turkey.

'He was sneaking around, spying on errant husbands and wives, boyfriends and girlfriends. He probably upset many people like that.'

'Upset them enough for them to set him on fire?'

'Who knows what a woman, or man, scorned is capable of?'

I stared at Jack, understanding that the pain of his marriage breakup would never leave him, no matter how many new relationships he'd have.

'And how does that connect to Betty Green? There was twenty years difference between them.'

He removed his finger from the table and shrugged.

'Hopefully, the team at the station will find something useful as they search through the files we found in Cole's office.'

'Hopefully.'

The food arrived, and the smell of fried bacon nearly knocked me off my chair. A large mug of tea came with it and, as I dropped two sugars into it, Jack bit through a piece of burnt toast. Most people would have spat it out, but I knew how much he loved it like that.

'Can I join you, Detective Inspectors?'

The man pulled up a seat and sat without waiting for an answer. He was about my height but with more flesh on his frame. His eyes glazed over at Jack's breakfast, and I assumed he'd had a few drinks before we'd got there. His long brown hair was tied into a ponytail, giving his angular head the appearance of a distracted horse. He took off his thick glasses, placed them on the table, and scratched at the scar under his cheek.

'Are you James Cole's associate?'

'Michael Ryan at your assistance, DI Flowers.'

I didn't ask how he knew me, but got straight to the point.

'Do you know of anyone who wanted to kill him?'

A member of the bar staff brought him a vegetarian breakfast as he considered the question. He stuck his fork into a meatless sausage, and then jabbed it between his lips, chewing on it as he replied.

'How much time have you got?'

Jack drowned his bacon in brown sauce. 'He had a lot of enemies?'

Ryan grabbed a tomato ketchup sachet and ripped it open with his teeth before squirting it across the river of beans in the middle of his plate.

'If you spend six days a week spying on infidelity, taking photos and videos of cheaters, you're going to make many people unhappy. And Jim made a lot of guys and gals unhappy.'

He reached for the mustard bottle as Jack did, their fingers bristling as my partner pulled his hand away and found the hot sauce instead. The two of them gripped their cutlery as if preparing for a duel, eyes fixed on each other across their plates. I finished my bacon sandwich and wiped my mouth.

'Do you think any of these people would be angry enough to set Cole on fire?'

Ryan picked a bit of tomato from his teeth, peered at it as if he'd been poisoned, and then placed it on the side of his plate.

'Has this got anything to do with that woman who was burnt to death the other day?'

Jack and I glanced at each other before I replied.

'What do you know about that?'

He licked his lips and shrugged. 'Only what I've read online.'

Jack dropped his knife on the table. 'So why bring it up?'

'It seemed very similar and I don't believe in coincidences.'

'That makes two of us, Mr Ryan,' I said. 'Did you or Mr Cole know that victim, Betty Green?'

He used a spoon to shovel the beans into his mouth.

'I'd never heard of her before reading the news, but I can't speak for Jim. He might have met her in his previous career.'

I took a drink from Jack's Coke, letting the bubbles tickle my throat before the next question.

'I thought he'd always been a private investigator?'

Ryan laughed out loud before unleashing an enormous burp. I flinched as the aroma reached me.

'Sorry, Inspector. Didn't you know he was a journalist before entering the murky world of spying on people?'

The ice from the drink sank into the abyss of my gut. But we hadn't known, which was sloppy on my part.

'What type of journalist?'

'Jim told me he'd been a crime reporter since he left university.' He grinned at an attractive woman half his age at the next table. 'He gave that up about ten years ago. He never said it in so many words, but I think he regretted it.'

Jack pushed his empty plate to the side. 'Which newspaper did he work for?'

'He was freelance; said he didn't like to be tied down to one spot. So one day, I asked him why he'd quit, but he gave me some flam about always wanting to be a PI.'

'How do you know it was flam?'

'I saw the pain in his eyes; that's how.' He glanced

around the room. 'Just like I can tell from his face that the bloke sitting on his own behind you only comes here because he's lonely. And that woman I smiled at will give me her phone number before I leave, even though I'm old enough to be her dad.' He stared at Jack. 'Just like I know your partner is thinking more about something else than your investigation.' Then he turned to me. 'And like I know you've got the weight of the world on your shoulders, Inspector.'

I returned his gaze. 'Are you a mind reader, Mr Ryan?'

He gripped his gut as he laughed. 'I wish I was. But, no, it's just years of experience in being able to read someone's expression. Not most people, of course; only those who can't help but wear their hearts on their sleeves. I'm sure you do something similar in your job, Inspector. Isn't that right?'

I answered his question with one of my own.

'Do you have a client list from Cole's business?'

He shook his head. 'I'm afraid not. Jim kept all his paperwork in the office.'

I stood to leave. 'What do you think I see when I look at you, Mr Ryan?'

He grinned at me. 'A handsome man wise beyond his years?'

It was my turn to shake my head. 'No. What I see is a lonely bloke desperately searching for meaning in his life.'

He kept on grinning as I left, his smile getting larger as he turned to the young woman at the next table.

Jack caught up with me outside. 'Wasn't that harsh, Jen?'

The street was full of noise and traffic as people hustled by.

'Cole was a journalist and quit ten years ago. Betty Green was a social worker and retired ten years ago.'

Jack removed his phone from his pocket. 'You think they're connected?'

'They have to be. You don't murder two people like that, in such a manner, without a link between them, even if it's only in the killer's mind.'

'You might be right.' He showed me the text on his mobile. 'Constable Grealish says she and Sutton have found something interesting.'

But she didn't say what.

So we returned to the station as I tried not to think about the approaching death of my ex-husband.

The doorbell rang as I made notes about the previous night's work. I knew it wasn't wise to record what I'd done, but it was cathartic and helped me focus on the next step in the plan. I left the notebook on the table and went to see who the visitor was. Perhaps it was someone from work checking up on me after I'd phoned in sick. The chain was still on the door as I inched it open.

'Pandora Lilly? I'm Sheila Smith from the Probation Services.'

'What happened to Dave?' I peered over Smith's shoulder.

'Dave left. I've taken over his clients.'

I shook my head. 'Clients, not ex-cons? How modern.'

Then I asked to see some identification. Smith searched through her bag, bending her head so I noticed the small butterfly tattoo on the back of her neck. She was a tiny woman, Napoleon sized, wearing a jacket too big for her and a white shirt with an egg stain on the collar. Once Smith showed me the ID card, I let her in.

She gazed at me as if scrutinising something terrible under a microscope. I raised a hand to my cheek, wondering if she could tell I was a murderer from the bags under my eyes or the lines crisscrossing my face like a poorly designed rail network.

Then I realised it was because of my clothes.

I was wearing a dead woman's top, something I'd picked up at the local charity shop. The sleeves were too short and they smelt of oranges. The jeans were as old as me and too tight, making my legs look as if they'd been transplanted from one of the Ramones. My slippers looked like hedgehogs and sent out a signal for people to keep away from me. Contact lenses had replaced thick glasses a year ago, but my teeth were still my own.

'Would you like a drink?' I said.

I gave Smith my best smile, trying to stay chipper until I saw my notebook on the table – my Murder Diary where I'd written everything I'd done to the social worker and the journalist. And my notes of what I was going to do next.

'I'm fine, thanks.' She inspected every inch of the room. 'Are you settling in okay, getting along with the neighbours?' Smith sat down on the sofa without an invitation, her hand close to the pages where I'd documented my murderous deeds. 'Dave wrote you'd had problems in your previous residence.'

I sat opposite the probation officer, keeping one eye on the notebook.

'Some people don't like having convicted criminals living near them. Every day they tell you what they think about you, always brim-full of fire and brimstone. Sometimes they'd write their thoughts down and stuff the paper through the door. They were hard to read through the shit, but I got the gist of it.'

'Well, that is unfortunate, but you're here now.'

She might have heard my words, but I guess they meant little to her.

'Yes, it's much better here.'

I gripped my leg, desperate to keep my fingers from shaking. Smith removed a writing pad from her bag and placed it on the table next to the Murder Diary. Her hair smelt of fried food, and something uncomfortable squirmed inside my guts. The probation officer put a pen near her lips and bit at the top as if she hadn't eaten all day. It seemed to go on forever, but it couldn't have been more than thirty seconds when she noticed me staring at her.

'I must stop doing that; it's such a filthy habit.'

She dropped the pen on the table next to her pad, but it rolled away and settled near the notebook. I jumped out of the sofa.

'I need a drink. Are you sure you don't want anything?'

'Well, if you have Coke, that would be great.' She pulled at the top of her shirt. 'It's warmer than I thought it would be.'

I nodded as I headed to the kitchen, stumbling inside, my hands shaking as if inside a blender. I pushed my shoulder into the wall, peering through the door to look at Smith and that notebook – my Murder Diary. I placed my palm on the counter to regain control, my fingers finding the large knife resting there. It was in my hand before I knew it, my skin feeling the caress of the handle, and then the blade.

If she looked inside the notebook, what would I do? Pretend it's all a fantasy, just some notes for a novel I'm writing? But the social worker's details are in there, plus how I'd found her and what happened in that house. And her name and the fire were all over the news. Smith would know that.

And Cole was all over those pages. There was even a sketch of what his face looked like as he went up in flames. One of the few things I was good for at school was art, something I'd improved during my time in prison.

The notebook – my Murder Diary – could also become an art book.

The blade was cold against my hand, a draught crawling over my face from the kitchen window. I listened to the traffic outside, the roar of accelerating cars, the voices mixing with the drums beating inside my skull.

If I waited too long, she'd look in the notebook. Then I'd have to kill her.

And I didn't want to do that for many reasons.

With paper-thin walls, the neighbours would hear what was going on in the flat. No matter how quick I was, she was bound to scream. Unless I could get behind her, run the knife across her throat with my other hand over her mouth. The blood would be everywhere and would be a devil to clean up. And how would I dispose of the body without anyone seeing me? I could cut her up in the bath, but it would be messy, and I didn't have the right tools for it. How long would it be before the neighbours complained about the smell?

I'd seen a story online once about an elderly man living alone who'd died in agony in a stinking flat. Somebody only called the police after the neighbours reported a horrendous stink coming from the flat.

Yes, the stink would be my undoing.

'Are you okay in there, Pandora?'

I dropped the knife, the metal rattling across the tiles.

'I'm fine.'

'You're not.'

She stood in the doorway, pointing at the blood dripping from me where the blade had cut me on its way to the floor. And I hadn't even felt it. I placed my bloodied fingers on the counter, opening a drawer to find the plasters.

'It's just a scratch, Ms Smith.'

My hand fumbled, finding discarded sweet wrappers, old clothes pegs, and a broken pencil amongst the plasters. There was no pain; my concentration focused on the interloper in my home.

Home? This was no home to me, only a waystation until I found what I wanted. At least Smith was away from the notebook. I grabbed a plaster and glanced into the living room.

The Murder Diary was gone.

I dropped the plaster to the floor, my legs following it down. I cracked my knee on the tiles, wincing as I did, watching my blood stain the kitchen as Smith bent to help me. The blade lay next to me, my fingers moving towards it.

I could do it now, thrust it into her stomach. It would be so easy. Then I could say it was an accident, that I dropped to the floor after cutting myself, the knife still in my hand – that she stumbled forward and fell into me and the blade. It sounded stupid, but I'd heard worse, especially in prison. I might get away with it.

But before I could do anything, Smith had dragged me up and was putting the plaster on my cut finger.

'It's not too bad. How's your knee?'

It throbbed as if plugged into Chernobyl just before it blew up. I ignored the pain and peered over Smith's shoulder into the living room.

Where had the notebook gone?

Had she taken it while I was in the kitchen, skimming

through it to see my death doodles and read what I'd done? She could have rung the police and they were already on their way here.

'I'm fine. I'll get you that Coke.'

I turned to the fridge and got two bottles, glasses, and ice. The cubes felt like heaven against my skin. I strode into the living room, sat and poured the drinks. My hand shook as I searched for the Murder Diary.

Smith slumped onto the sofa opposite.

Was she playing with me, gazing at me because she believed criminals could never be reformed?

She grabbed her writing pad, opened it, and started making notes as she drank.

'I guess a bit of excitement is a good way to start the day.'

I nodded, slurping at the Coke as my fingers throbbed, steadying myself to answer all of Smith's questions about adapting to the outside world after ten years inside.

'I've been out for six months.'

I fixed on the probation officer's eyes, scrutinising them to see if she had the notebook.

'That's true, but you've moved accommodation once and, well, the country has changed a lot in a decade. So there are many things you have to get used to, and that's difficult for anybody.'

And it's even worse for an ex-con.

She didn't say the words, but I saw them lingering in her eyes.

But she wasn't wrong. To me, the world had become crueller, less tolerant, and harder for those existing in the margins to survive.

Not that I was going to tell her that.

'I've always been good at adapting.'

Smith glanced up from her notes. 'So I see from your records.' She lifted the pen to her lips again, but stopped halfway to her mouth. 'I'm sorry, but I have to ask if you've associated with anyone involved in criminal activity in the last month?'

Does the person in the mirror count? I didn't say that to her.

I finished my drink. 'No. Apart from work, I hardly leave the flat.'

Smith shut her pad and dropped the pen into her pocket. 'Okay, that's enough for now.'

She was about to stand before hesitating, reaching underneath the table for something I couldn't see. But I guessed what it was.

My Murder Diary.

Smith grabbed the diary and stood.

My fingers twitched; I wished I'd brought the knife with me. I didn't want to kill her, but I would if there was no other choice.

'I'm sorry. I knocked this on the floor earlier when I heard you shout in the kitchen.'

My brain told me to grab it, but I couldn't with the shakes returning to my hand. Was it true what she'd said? Maybe she was reading it when it fell from her fingers.

I smiled and took it. 'Thank you. I only use it for my recipes.'

Smith returned the smile. 'That's good that you have a hobby. We can't have you here on your own, dwelling on the past, can we? It's nice you have something to keep you busy. Perhaps next time, you'll show me what you cook.'

'Of course.' Fried flesh with a side dish of revenge, best served cold. 'It will be my pleasure, Ms Smith.'

I showed her out of the flat, my body in desperate need

of a drink more substantial than Coke. But I delayed that satisfaction, slumping into the sofa instead.

Then I opened the Murder Diary and revelled in my work once more.

22 JEN: THE FLAT

I told Sutton to get the keys to Cole's flat and meet us there. Whatever she'd discovered could wait half an hour until she could tell us in person. So Jack and I walked there from the pub, a gentle stroll through Camden apart from all the noise crammed into my head: Ray's terminal illness; the money he was leaving for Abbey and how that would affect her; her interest in her father and what I should tell her; how she was going to fit her schoolwork in with the music and the football; my mother and her claim I was adopted. And if I might hallucinate my father's voice again. In addition, there was someone who had burnt two people to death.

'Didn't you spend your teenage years around here, Jen?'

I peered across at the market, watching the sellers and taking in the aromas of the street: the smell of fresh bread, fried chicken, sizzling tomatoes, and cakes sweeter than a mountain of sugar. The sounds drifted over and through me: the chatter of buying and selling; teenage girls singing pop songs unknown to me; and a stall full of Jamaican products, food and clothes, where the owner was playing reggae's greatest hits. I had a

sudden temptation to kick off my shoes, find a beach and a cocktail bar, and then sip on tequila cocktails for the rest of the day.

Instead, I answered Jack's question.

'Some of them. I lived around here during my studies,
and the nightlife always drew you in.'

'Were you with Ray, then?'

My legs froze and I stopped. Not because of his question, but to wait while a giant of a man carrying a placard
declaring WE'RE ALL GOING TO BURN IN HELL
pushed by. Fire and brimstone fell from his mouth, plus a
few choice words we could have arrested him for. But I let
him go and started walking again. Cole's flat was nearby.

'It was my first year as a copper. He frequented the
same places as me, and he was always very popular.'

'And you weren't?'

'I kept myself to myself most of the time. I had a few
mates, but I never felt comfortable around large groups.'

I still didn't. And what had happened to those friends? I
remembered their names, but the faces were a blur.

We strode past The Roundhouse and I heard James
Brown's voice in my head again. Three minutes later, we
were outside Cole's flat. Constable Sutton was already
there, speaking to someone I assumed to be a neighbour.
Sarah had the keys in her hand.

'I've got something to show you, ma'am.'

I pointed at the door. 'Let's do it inside.'

She nodded and took us in. It was a modern two-
bedroom flat, with a recent lick of paint. A forensic team
had visited yesterday, removing a laptop and mobile phone,
and we were still waiting on Cybercrime's report on those.
It was whiter than a hospital corridor and spotlessly clean,
smelling of fresh lemon.

Jack scanned the full bookshelf against the back wall of the living room.

'Spying on people must have been a decent payday.'

I left him to check the rooms and spoke to Sutton.

'What have you found, Sarah?'

'I've been digging through his online presence. Did you know he used to be a journalist?'

I nodded. 'We do now.'

'Well, I started on his website, but there's nothing unusual there. So then I searched through his social media connections and I discovered this.'

She handed me her phone.

'What am I looking at, Sarah?'

'He doesn't have a personal Facebook page, but he set this up five years ago for the private investigation business. It looks like he hardly used it, but there are a few good luck comments at the beginning from people he must have known or worked with in the media. And I found that at the bottom.'

I scrolled down the screen to the first comment posted on the page.

All the best, mate.

It was from someone named Dan Crow.

'Is this guy significant, Sarah?'

She shook her head. 'I'm not sure, ma'am. I haven't had time to check him yet, but what got my attention was who had liked that post.'

I peered at the words, and then the tiny thumbs-up symbol below them. I pressed my finger into it to see what Constable Sutton meant.

LIKED BY BETTY GREEN

I returned the phone to Sutton.

'Is that our Betty Green?' I assumed there would be hundreds across the country.

'I'm guessing so, but I don't know for definite. The account it was posted from is dormant, used only for that post five years ago. I've passed the information on to Cyber-crime, so maybe they'll get more from it.'

Jack stepped into the living room. 'What did I miss?' Sutton showed him the Facebook post and explained it to him. 'So, there is a connection between them?'

Sutton retrieved her phone from him. 'It looks like it, sir.'

'Well, that's something. Perhaps it's connected to what I found in the bedroom.'

We followed him in and stared at the dozen shoeboxes.

'Where did you find these?' I said.

'Under the bed, in the cupboard, and on the wardrobe. He didn't hide them.'

I slipped on plastic gloves and sat close to a box on the bed. Then I removed the top bits of newspaper clippings and read them. Sarah and Jack did the same with the other boxes. The first one in my hand was from twenty years ago, all yellowed and smelling like an old pair of trousers. I held it up to the light streaming through the window and scanned the details. Then I did the same to half a dozen others from that box while Jack and Sarah followed suit with their collections.

'These are all reports he's written for newspapers.' I dropped them back into the box, sensing the ink from the paper staining my hand through the gloves even though that was impossible. 'How old was Cole?'

Sutton replied. 'Forty-five, ma'am.'

I nudged the box away from my leg. 'From what I read,

he must have filed articles with most of the major national newspapers.'

'And quite a few of the London locals,' Jack said, 'going by what I went through.'

'Were they all crime related reports?' I said.

They both nodded.

Jack put his hand on the side of the nearest box. 'It seems he covered everything from drug trafficking to murder.'

I looked at Sutton.

'It was the same in the pile I read, ma'am: prostitution, gangland shootings, robbery, and GBH.'

The boxes and their contents appeared to whisper to me as I glanced across them.

'There must be something in these, in his crime articles, which links him to Betty Green.'

'And our killer,' Jack said.

He was right. And there were likely twenty years of reports in the surrounding boxes. I turned to Sutton.

'Get some reinforcements and a van over here, Sarah, so we can go through these at the station.'

She was on her phone before I finished. 'Yes, ma'am.'

I returned to the living room, and Jack followed me.

'Did you check the other rooms?' I said.

'I did. There's nothing unusual in the bathroom or the kitchen, while the second bedroom is full of books, records and CDs. And a few clothes.'

I stepped into that room, expecting everything he mentioned to be littered everywhere in chaos, but it was the exact opposite: the lot was stacked on shelves, organised in alphabetical order, without a spot of dust anywhere. The carpet looked like it was hoovered yesterday and the bed was tidy. I moved to the books and removed one from the middle of the shelf.

'*Farewell, My Lovely* by Raymond Chandler.'

Jack took it from me. 'Perhaps he used it for research when he started his PI business.'

'He'd have been better off reading some P D James.' I left him with the book and looked through Cole's CD collection: mainly American gospel music. And then I spotted the James Brown album at the end, and I thought someone was playing tricks on me. I flicked the CD over and looked through the track listing, finding one of my favourites: *Stoned to the Bone.*

'Do you think we should have all this shipped to the station as well, Jen?'

I returned the CD to the same spot I'd lifted it from. 'No. Hopefully, we'll find something in those clippings.'

'What about that Facebook post? Could that be the same Betty Green murdered in a similar fashion to Cole?'

'How old was she, sixty? So there was an age gap between them, but maybe he met her when he worked as a freelance journalist.'

'Covering crime in London? How would that bring him into contact with social services and Green?'

'Social services deal with shady characters all the time, Jack; we both know this. So perhaps Cole was chasing down a story, and it led him to Green.'

'If that's the case, we need to find out what that story was.'

We returned to the living room, where Constable Sutton had taken a box and placed it on the table. She was going through the papers again, engrossed in that old text.

'Have you discovered anything useful?' I said.

She dropped the papers into the box. 'Not yet, ma'am. Cole's writing style is absorbing.'

I walked to her. 'His writing style?'

'Yes. He had a real talent for getting to the heart of a story and making it gripping. It's a shame he gave up journalism.'

A shame indeed, in more ways than one.

'If he was that good, why did he quit?' Jack said. 'And why did Betty Green take early retirement at the same time? From what I can gather, from those who worked with her, she loved that job. They said it was all she had in her life.'

'Perhaps they were both forced out,' I said.

Jack narrowed his eyes. 'Threatened?' I nodded. 'But with what and why?'

'Those are excellent questions, partner.' I glanced towards the door as two uniformed officers entered. I left Sarah to organise the removal of the boxes. 'I'm sure once we find the answers to them, we'll be closer to identifying the killer.'

Constable Sutton handed the box on the table to one of her colleagues and turned to me.

'What if they weren't threatened, but paid off, ma'am?'

'Bribed?' I said.

'Yes. Green had money that couldn't have been from her pension. We know this from what the neighbours said about her taking three or four foreign holidays a year. And it seems like Cole didn't work for five years after quitting journalism and before setting up his PI business. So the cash must have come from somewhere.'

I was considering what she'd said when I received a text.

'Whatever it was, bribery or threats, there must be a

connection between the two of them,' Jack said. 'We just need to find that link to be one step closer to the killer.'

I nodded in agreement as I checked my phone. Abbey had a match in an hour and wanted me to go to it. How could I say no to that?

Text me the location and I'll see you soon.

Then I spoke to my partner.

'Can I leave you to organise the boxes, and we'll start on them tomorrow? I have to watch Abbey kick a football around a muddy field.'

'Sure, Jen.' He grinned at me. 'Don't start any arguments with the other parents.'

He joked, but it gave me an idea of how to kill two birds with one stone.

All I had to do was make a quick stop on the way to the match.

23 PANDORA: THE CELEBRATION

I waited in the doctors' reception, sitting between the man with gout and the woman who looked like she was about to give birth to quads. It was a strange experience, considering they were there on my last visit. For one second, I imagined it was a waking dream or a *déjà vu* until I guessed I was feeling dizzy from my lack of medication. My painkillers were so intense, I had to see the doctor once a month to get them.

Plus, I'd received an exciting invite for tonight, so I had to show enthusiasm in trying to get better before leaving the house later. Or at least have a doctor's note as evidence for the relevant people.

This time, I got the older doctor, Dr Murphy, and I wasn't happy about it. Murphy was about seventy, going by the wrinkles making up his face. He scrutinised me from behind bottle-bottom glasses, and I knew he was judging me. But the younger ones like Dr Ruth were more up to date with their methods and the realisation the world had moved on beyond the 1950s. Or at least London had.

Dr Ruth would talk to me about the latest Netflix shows

and what was trending on Twitter. She even had a TikTok page. Murphy would mutter under his breath, usually about the scandal of single mothers or how to rid the streets of the homeless, while writing out my prescription. I felt playful after turning into shit this morning, so I got my jabs in first.

'My breasts are too big, Doctor.'

It made him lift his head from the paperwork. He'd signed it, so I removed it from the desk before he changed his mind.

'What did you say?'

I pushed my chest towards him in a *Carry On* fashion.

'I think that's why I'm in so much pain. The weight of them is throwing my posture out.'

Ooh, Matron, I wanted to say, but didn't, the image of my Murder Diary falling into the wrong hands still playing inside my head. He glared at me and shoved his glasses so far up his nose, I thought they might crack.

'You said the pain was from the scars on your back, from the...'

I cut him off before he could finish.

'Yes, Doctor, they're always hurting me, but I think my breasts are making it worse. Perhaps you should examine them.'

His glasses steamed up. 'Is that what you want?'

I couldn't tell if the prospect excited or frightened him. Maybe it was a bit of both. I grinned and got up.

'Perhaps next month,' I waved the prescription at him, 'if these don't work.'

My heart fluttered as I left, the skin tingling across my arms as if I'd walked underneath some low-hanging electrical pylons. There was energy in the air and I'd forgotten my morning melancholy. Now I had to return home and prepare for an evening's entertainment.

TWO DAYS after my surprise celebration at work, I was at another surprising gathering. Gladys and her brother had given me a lift to this party. I'd said I was fine taking the bus, but she wouldn't take no for an answer, which I assumed was her way of trying to set me up with her brother, Frank.

Cans of deodorant and hairspray littered the floor of the car. It also had a lingering aroma of mouldy plastic clinging to everything, and the leather seats seemed to have been ripped open with a serrated knife.

I stared at Frank's reflection in the mirror, imaging him as a deranged drug runner, even though Gladys had told me he was a bricklayer for the council. He had a face for mixing concrete. At least the sounds in the car were great, a mix of electronic dance and pop I hadn't heard in an age.

She relaxed as we travelled to the party, showing me a different side to her. She was quite a talker, changing the music while gabbing, and then starting imaginary conversations with people she saw in the streets. She would ask them a question, then answer it from her point of view. I hardly said a word, fascinated by her behaviour.

When we arrived at the venue, I spoke, having to answer Gladys's question regarding if I'd got in touch with the dancing police officer from the other day.

I'd never called that phone number, but she'd clicked with the other fake copper so quickly it was her engagement party we were attending. I wondered who would be the first to tell Gladys she was rushing into things, but when I saw how happy she was, I kept my thoughts on marriage to myself.

She was no spring chicken; a spinster or old maid would have been her title in the past, and it was true her personality was about as sparkling as ten-year-old Bucks Fizz, so perhaps this would be the best she'd ever do.

I wondered what sort of reception I'd get when I arrived since I'd missed a workday without a good excuse. But I needn't have worried as all everyone did was check to see if I was feeling better. Even Bob seemed concerned, telling me to take as much time off as needed. From the anxious look on his face, I guessed he thought it was my mental health which had wobbled and not anything physical. And he wasn't wrong. But I put that behind me and focused on why I was there – to help Gladys celebrate.

The fiancé's name was Marc, spelt with a lone C as he told people all night, and he was at least twenty years younger than Gladys's half-century. I spoke to him only once during the festivities as he busied himself entertaining all the guests. I assumed he'd ask about my intentions towards his friend, the other fake copper, named Rudolph.

'You know, like the reindeer,' Marc said.

Or Valentino, I thought. *Or Hess.*

But he didn't ask about his mate, only mentioning him in passing as he waxed lyrical about how much he was smitten with the vivacious Gladys.

'It's love at first sight,' they both told me several times.

So I spent a few hours whiling away the night, finding it somewhat dull until I discovered my favourite gin was on special offer. After a few doubles – I lost count after four – it increased my appreciation of the occasion.

Close to eleven o'clock, I was standing outside the pub, waiting for my taxi, when a husky voice spoke up.

'I told him to take his time, but he won't listen to me. I mean, Gladys is lovely and all, but this has happened too quickly, don't you think?'

Rudolph was no reindeer, but his nose was red, from either the cold or what he'd had to drink. Or both.

'As long as they're both happy.'

Wasn't that the most important thing: finding joy, no matter the cost? Even if that cost was unhappiness, or worse, for others?

What I was doing wasn't about happiness, but justice. Some might call it revenge, but I knew better. It was the truth I sought. And I also realised I couldn't let anything distract me from uncovering that truth.

He lit a match and offered me a cigarette. I declined, but the heat from the match warmed my cheek and resurrected memories of my recent actions. The night air disappeared around me, the smell of the match filling my senses with the scent of burning flesh. It had been unpleasant at first, but I was getting accustomed to it.

My taxi arrived and I left him smoking behind me. Perhaps when this was all over, I could think of romance again.

I doubted it, but it was good to hope.

My detour didn't take as long as I'd expected, so I arrived at Hampstead before the teams had taken to the pitch. At least there was no rain, but a nagging doubt battered the insides of my head: I hoped my surprise wouldn't affect Abbey's game.

During my wait for that surprise, I spent the time on my phone, researching curious facts about women's football in Britain so I'd have something to talk to Abbey about later. The women's game had a long history in the country, with one website claiming the most famous 16th-century female spectator was Mary, Queen of Scots. Perhaps that was the real reason Queen Bess had her cousin's head chopped off – because they'd supported different teams. I imagined that as my guest was escorted to the car.

And now we were standing on the sidelines, feet in the mud, waiting for the girls to take centre stage. Finally, a hundred years after The Football Association banned its members from allowing women's football to be played at their grounds – killing the women's game overnight, Abbey and a bunch of other girls could think of a professional career in the sport. Rigsby seemed to believe Abbey had a good chance of that, and who was I to argue with her?

I didn't know whether the match was important beyond an ordinary game, but a large crowd had gathered, with perhaps sixty or seventy people there. On the other side, I recognised someone from the other match I'd attended: Grace Randolph. Her wealthy husband wasn't there, though I guessed the wealth was hers too since they were married. Instead, there was a massive entourage with her, including a muscular bloke about six foot four who must have been a bodyguard.

As I observed them, my singular entourage spoke up.

'Why have you dragged me out here in the cold?'

She glared at me through icy eyes. The longer I stared at her, the more I wondered if it was my future I peered at, which made me yearn for that brief period when I'd thought I might have been adopted.

'Don't you want to meet your granddaughter, Mother?'

The authorities at the care home had jumped at the idea of me taking her out when I rang them, but she'd needed convincing. I'd believed the thought of meeting Abbey would spur her into action and was surprised when she cringed at the suggestion; until I remembered she thought I wasn't her biological daughter, which meant Abbey wasn't blood-related to her either. I think it was just the temptation of getting out of that building that persuaded her to accompany me.

'Couldn't I have met her in a restaurant? Even a Pizza Hut would do.'

'If you behave, we might go for something after the game, before I take you home.'

'Home!' She spat the word into the grass. 'That's not my home, you stupid cow. My home was with your father.'

Now she'd returned to admitting I was her daughter. But it was him I was interested in.

'Do you know where he is, my father?'

She gazed at her fingers as if they were worms wriggling on hooks.

'He'll be back, don't you worry. And you'll know when it happens. He always knew what you were up to.'

The weather was calm, but a storm was brewing inside my head.

'And what was I up to, Mother?'

She twisted her lips and wagged a wrinkled finger at me.

'You know what, with you messing around with that poor man from the church.'

My nails dug into my palm so much, I thought my hand would split in two.

'Do you remember how old I was when this happened, Mother?'

She rubbed at her forehead and avoided my gaze. 'It doesn't matter now.' She glanced at the girls as they came out of the changing rooms. 'I just hope this girl of yours is better than that.'

That girl of mine ran out in front of her teammates, waving at me as she went. I watched her glance at the woman next to me, noticing the recognition on her face. She smiled before taking the ball from the referee and kicking it on to the pitch.

'What's up, Ms Flowers?'

Francine sidled up to me, her hand covered in a bandage, her head buried inside a hood.

'What happened to you, Francine?'

She held the damaged hand up to me. 'This, it's nothing. The other girls think I'm doing it just to avoid playing, but they're stupid. I fell downstairs and fractured my wrist, that's all.'

Before I could reply, my mother stepped forward.

'Who hit you in the face, girl?'

'What?' Francine raised her unbandaged fingers to her mouth.

My mother pointed to her.

'Someone punched you in the face. I recognise a black eye when I see it. You can dump as much muck on your mug as you want, but you can't hide that.' My mother glanced at me. 'Not from me, anyway.'

I pushed her to the side to stand right in front of Francine, cursing my blindness for not noticing the damage to her eye the other day. No wonder she had so much makeup on.

The whistle went behind me to start the game.

'What happened to you, Francine?'

She shook her head. 'Nothing, Ms Flowers. I stumbled down the stairs, that's all.' Her voice trembled along with the rest of her.

'How many times did you fall down the stairs?'

Her eyes glazed over, the distress consuming her face, but not enough to hide the damage anymore.

'It was just an accident, Ms Flowers, I promise you.'

I wanted to grab hold of Francine and shake some sense into her, my head full of noise and confusion. The crowd was shouting, and Abbey stuck the ball into the net as I looked up. I watched her run towards us, followed by her teammates as they tried to catch her. She slid through the mud with her arms in the air, a giant smile on her face. Then she got up and sprinted back to the middle of the pitch. By the time I turned from her, both Francine and my mother had gone.

'Fuck!'

The noise increased inside my skull like a jackhammer pounding at the front of my brain. I looked from side to side, seeing Francine going in one direction while my mother went in the other. It wasn't much of a choice which one I'd go after.

I followed her from the pitch towards the group gathered around Grace Randolph. They were hanging on Randolph's every word as if she was giving a TED Talk on how to improve your life. And then my mother spoke up.

'Why don't you do something useful with yourself, Randolph?'

The multi-millionaire's wife stopped talking, touched her cheek, and turned to my mother.

'What would you suggest?'

My mother glanced at the game going on behind her, ignoring me, before returning to her audience.

'Stop wasting money on games and spend it helping people, like the homeless or runaway kids. Your husband owns plenty of empty properties, so why don't you sweet-talk him into using some of them for the good of local communities?'

I could only stand there, gobsmacked. She was as clear-headed and as sane as I'd ever seen her. Where had she got all this information on the Randolphs?

A tall blonde woman stepped away from the crowd and approached my mother.

'You should mind your own business, lady. Mrs Randolph does lots of work with local communities and charities.' As I got to them, the heat from the woman's face warmed the air. 'She's always helping young kids with training and education. And she helps those who need somewhere to stay get places in a youth hostel.'

My mother wagged a finger at her. 'Lady – if you even are one – every time you speak, you lose a brain cell.' She grinned at the woman. 'You look like a two dollar whore that would be a waste of a dollar ninety-five.'

Randolph's defender simmered, her face resembling an inflated tangerine. I grabbed my mother's arm and dragged her back, with no attempt to hide my anger.

'What are you doing?'

She shook herself from my grasp. 'Leave me alone, woman. Who are you?'

The group stared at us as I looked from her to them. Grace Randolph peered at me, her eyes full of intrigue. I tried to explain to her what had happened.

'I'm sorry, Mrs Randolph. My mother has a few problems with her memory.'

Randolph strode towards me through the crowd, the people parting as if waiting for Moses to march through the Red Sea.

'Perhaps you should get her out of this cold weather.' She touched her cheek as if it was on fire. 'It's very harsh on the skin.'

'She's not taking me anywhere.' Mother glared at me. 'I don't know who she is,' she switched to Randolph, 'but I know you, with all your money and how you waste it.'

I grabbed her arm again, more forcefully this time, and dragged her back to Abbey's football match. I expected her to struggle, but she didn't, instead muttering obscenities under her breath, which I couldn't hear above the laughter coming from the group which had surrounded Randolph once more.

She relaxed in my grip, her irritation gone.

'Can we get something to eat, Jenny? I'm starving.'

I stopped walking and let go of her. Confusion consumed her face, and a chill snapped at my heart.

'When Abbey finishes her game, the three of us will eat together.'

Her lips wobbled as she spoke. 'Is Abbey the one with the black eye?'

'No, Mother, that's Francine. Abbey is your grand-daughter.'

'Granddaughter? I don't have a granddaughter. You killed the baby, remember?'

She strode past me towards the pitch, leaving me standing there catching flies. I was frozen to the spot for an eternity, but it must have been less than a minute. When I moved and caught up with her, the crowd was cheering another Abbey goal.

I stood next to my mother until the end of the game with no word between us. Then we waited for Abbey to come out. I looked for Francine, but didn't see her. My mother hummed an Abba tune to herself, the same song on repeat until Abbey appeared.

Then I did the introductions.

'Abbey, this is your grandmother, Ruth. Mother, this is Abbey.'

They stared at each other in silence until my daughter threw her arms around my mother.

'Hello, Grandma.'

I watched my mother, wary of her reaction. But I had nothing to worry about.

'Hello, Abbey. It's nice to meet you finally.' She grinned at my daughter before letting go of her. Then she turned to me. 'So, where are you taking us to eat, Jenny?'

TWENTY MINUTES LATER, we were at McDonald's. It was Abbey's favourite place and the first visit for my mother, who appeared to love it. I bought her a cheeseburger, fries, and Coke. She studied the burger as if it was food flown in from a different planet.

'This cheese is wonderful, all melty and cheesy.'

I left her to enjoy it and spoke to Abbey. 'What was the final score?'

'8–1. We slacked off for the last fifteen minutes, but that's okay cos we have another game on Saturday morning.'

'Did you see Francine?'

Was this the time to mention her best friend's black eye and ask how she'd got it? And then there was her fractured wrist.

Abbey avoided my gaze. 'I didn't see her.' The barbecue sauce was sticking to her lips. 'I think she had an accident at home.'

'Somebody smacked her around.' My mother slurped on her drink. 'That poor kid's in trouble.'

I stared at my daughter and waited for a reaction, but she stayed quiet. So I asked the question.

'Is Francine in trouble, Abbey?'

She chewed on her paper straw. 'I told you, Mum. She had an accident. You know what Franny's like; she's always clumsy, banging into things and tripping up. She'll be fine.'

Abbey was right about Francine's clumsiness: I'd once seen her trip over the cat in our living room, and another time she'd walked into a lamppost outside the house. But I also had a suspicion there was some truth in what my mother had said. So I was considering what to do about it when Mother dropped a handful of fries on the floor and stared at the empty table next to us.

'I used to enjoy football, you know.' She gazed at Abbey. 'George Best took me out once.'

Best had been dead for a while, but I didn't mention that, thinking it better to humour her.

'Where did you go?'

'To a pub.'

'Did you like him?'

'No, I didn't!'

'Why not?'

'He wouldn't buy me a drink.'

'When was this?'

'Last week.'

I finished my food and watched her staring into space. Abbey didn't appear to be fazed by her grandmother's difficulties, but this wasn't the place to talk about it. It could wait until after I dropped my mother at the nursing home. And perhaps I'd ask about Francine.

'Are you ready to go back, Mother?'

She peered into my eyes, picked up a napkin and folded it in half.

'This is my job,' she said. 'I do it every day. I like to keep things neat.' Her face was expressionless until the moment the napkin slipped from her and unfolded – then she grinned. 'I'm not doing a very good job, am I?'

I smiled and took her hand. 'You just need to practise, Mother. We can do it again when Abbey and I visit you.'

Her skin was warm against mine as her eyes lit up.

'I'd like that.' She glanced between Abbey and me. 'Who are you again?'

I gripped her fingers, attempting to remove my memories as she'd lost hers.

Then I took her back and questioned what I'd do with both my mother and daughter.

25 PANDORA: THE REPORTS

W ork had been dull, my mind unable to contain the information I'd got from the failed journalist and prompting me to do something about it. But I couldn't, not yet. It was too soon. The next one would be much more capable of handling themselves than the other two.

So I struggled through a boring day in the office before feasting on microwave fish and chips when I got home. Then I forced myself to watch a TV show where other people watched TV shows, and then offered their illuminating opinions on what they'd seen. I was slumped on the sofa, resembling a large uncooked potato for most of the night.

Sleep was beyond me, so I cleaned the kitchen and bathroom before hoovering the carpets. Then I rearranged all the tins in the cupboards in alphabetical order. Unfortunately, some were at least two weeks out of date, but I kept them anyway.

After that, I got my secret paperwork and a beer before settling into the living room. The TV was on with the sound on mute, the screen displaying an old black and white Marx Brothers film from the thirties.

I pushed the Murder Diary to the other side of my drink and reached for the folder I'd retrieved from under the bed. I sipped on the booze as I removed a group of papers. The first was a report from my first foster home when I was four-teen. I'd stolen it from my social worker's office all those years ago and must have read it more than a hundred times. I kept it to remind myself of the person I once was.

The alcohol warmed me as I scanned the report once again.

Pandora's relationship with the Smith children is chal-lenging. Twice she's been caught fighting with the oldest daughter Caroline (14). Mrs Smith found Pandora in the garden, pinning Caroline to the floor and trying to stuff dirt into her mouth. Pandora had been in the home for two months. When asked about her behaviour, she said she was only defending herself. However, Caroline claimed she was attacked.

Caroline had lied. I'd found her in my bedroom going through my clothes, looking for God knows what since I had nothing of value. That's when I saw she was wearing gloves and sticking shit in the pockets of my trousers.

So I lost my mind and beat the crap out of her. None of the adults believed me when I told them what had happened.

The next part of the report was more serious.

On a separate occasion, a group of children gathered around the girls as they fought in the street. Witnesses said Caroline was screaming at Pandora, calling her a liar when she'd accused Caroline's father of entering Pandora's bedroom as she was undressing. Mr Smith denied the claim.

He did it most nights, always pretending to be looking

out for me. Caroline's father only stopped when I kicked him in the balls. He was naked, lunging for me as I came out of the bathroom. Nobody believed me again, but I wondered if Caroline knew what he was like and if he'd done the same with her.

Pandora was verbally abusive to Mr Smith daily, some of which was recorded on camera. Pandora can be seen and heard swearing at Mr Smith in the video clips.

This was all true, but I had good reason.

Pandora fainted on more than one occasion, and Mrs Smith took her to the hospital. The doctors found nothing untoward with her.

They didn't really check. The nurses were okay with me, but the doctors were always blokes, and they looked at me as if I was distracting them from something more important. The fainting stopped after a while, but I was suspicious that Smith might have been doping me.

Sometimes, Pandora refused to eat with the family and wouldn't give a reason why.

Not one of several social workers could understand why I did this.

The continuing difficulties for Pandora in the Smith household led to her removal and placement in a residential care home. Pandora's behaviour and school reports improved in the immediate aftermath.

I placed the comments face down on the table and scanned through the other papers: the note from a teacher praising me for my hard work, diligence, and dedication. I didn't know what diligence meant then. I lay that next to the report from my first visit to the police station, a constable's notes on when I was caught shoplifting a pair of shoes and a handbag from Primark.

The girl is insolent and rude to a degree I've never seen

before. She's antagonistic to all forms of authority and is quick to temper. There are marks on both wrists, which may have been self-inflicted. Pandora needs to see a doctor ASAP, with a recommendation to a child psychologist at the earliest opportunity.

I spent two teenage years, fourteen to sixteen, with weekly visits to a psychologist. Sometimes I stole the notes she made, adding them to my collection.

The death of Pandora's parents when she was twelve has affected her deeply. These effects didn't manifest immediately, but appeared gradually over the following six months of her time in care under social services. Her behaviour is problematic and challenging, which increased when she lived with a foster family. Pandora was removed from there and returned to a residential care home.

Pandora's erratic behaviour is a cry for help in dealing with her parents' death. However, she finds acceptance and encouragement at school. She has at least one friend there who she relies on and trusts.

I rarely think of my parents now unless I'm reading these papers. They lay on the table as artefacts of a past that never leaves me. Some might say I should destroy them and focus on the present and what I'll achieve in the future, but there's only one path I can take going forward.

I returned the psychologist's notes to the folder and turned to my Murder Diary. I'd learnt to love writing when I was at school, but found little time for it when I left; living on the streets didn't foster a progressive, creative environment. It was only when I was behind bars that I had the opportunity to write again, to find solace in the workings of my imagination. It didn't matter that the Murder Diary was evidence of my crimes; all I cared about was what it gave me.

It peered at me, so I reached over and picked it up, turning to the first blank page, a pen in my hand as I wrote the name of the next person on my list. Once I'd spoken to him, I'd be able to rest.

Then I'd know what happened to her.

Let it go, Mum. It's not too late.

Her voice had never left me, even if she had.

Abbey was about to leave for school when I got downstairs.

'Give me five minutes, love, and I'll drop you off.' I poured myself a cup of coffee.

'There's no need, Mum. I'm going to Francine's first.'

The drink was lukewarm, so I drank half in one go, the bitter taste grafting itself to my throat.

'That's okay, Abbey. I'll take you there.'

She lifted a hand towards me in what I expected to be a protest, but she dropped it as quickly as it was raised.

'Haven't you got work to do at the station?'

'Sure. But that can wait. I need to speak to Francine's mother and father.'

The shimmer in her eyes turned to fire.

'What for?'

'You know why, Abbey.' I finished the drink and grabbed my jacket. 'I want to talk to her parents about these accidents she's had. Perhaps there's some medical condition at play here.'

She continued to glare at me. 'Would you want

someone coming around here and telling you how to look after me?'

'If there was a problem, then yes.'

She snorted laughter, grabbed her bag, and left. I got my car keys and followed her.

We completed the drive in silence, apart from the music on the radio. I let her choose the station, so we were serenaded by teenagers singing about lost love or putting the world to rights.

'What are you going to say?' Abbey said when we arrived.

It was a good question. How delicately could I put it if I thought someone was harming their daughter? And by someone, I was implying it was one of them.

I switched off the engine. 'Wait here. I won't be long.'

It was eight in the morning and the street was empty. I walked up the path and rang the bell. It was the first time I'd been to the house, but I'd spoken to Mrs West, Ella, on the phone many times. They weren't in-depth conversations with get-to-know-you questions, just two mothers making sure their daughters were okay. This meant I knew little about her or the husband apart from them being a few years younger than me in their early thirties. I might have heard Abbey say once that Francine's father was a shoe salesman, but I could have been wrong.

I glanced back at Abbey as the door opened. The woman who greeted me looked ten years older than I'd expected and had a brand new bruise under her eye. So fresh, I guessed she'd received it in the last few hours.

'Mrs West, I'm Abbey's mum, Jen. We've spoken on the phone before.'

Her eyes were dull as if all the life had been sucked out

of them. She offered her hand to me and I noticed the scratches along her arm.

'Jen, yes. How nice to finally meet you.'

I took her hand and smiled. Then I let go as she moved in the doorway as if to hide something behind her.

'Is anything wrong, Ella?' I said.

Her lips trembled as she spoke.

'Oh, no, the house is a mess, that's all. You know how it is, not wanting people to see the place when it's not tidy.' She glanced over my shoulder at the car. 'Have you come to take Franny to school?' She shook her head. 'I'm afraid she's not feeling well, so I'm keeping her home.'

'You don't look too well yourself, Ella. What happened to your face?'

She lifted shaky fingers to her cheek.

'This... this is nothing. I walked into the wardrobe when I was half asleep. I'm such a klutz. I think that's where Franny gets it from.'

'She's had quite a few accidents lately, hasn't she? A black eye and a fractured wrist.'

Ella West folded her arms. 'Yes, well, you know what teenagers are like, Jen, always getting up to no good, and with Franny being so clumsy, it's just a recipe for disaster.'

Defiance flowed from her now. Gone were the shakes and the nerves. Could I leave her like this? As I considered that, a loud crash came from behind her. She turned and ran inside, allowing me to follow her into the living room.

Broken glass lay scattered on the floor in front of a table; it looked as if a mirror had fallen off the wall. I pulled her back as she stepped towards it, noticing she wore nothing on her feet.

'Be careful, Ella.'

Her eyes were like a rabbit on the shooting range.

'Where's Franny?' She squirmed out of my grasp and ran out of the room. 'Franny, are you okay?'

She was up the stairs before I could move. I stared at the glass, then at the gap on the wall where the mirror had been. There were two nails secured into the stone, undamaged. Someone must have dragged it off and thrown it down.

I left the damage and went upstairs, finding her in what I assumed was Francine's bedroom. Posters of musicians I didn't recognise covered the walls, and books and CDs stood stacked on creaking shelves. She was sitting on the bed, cradling a stuffed toy resembling David Bowie in his Ziggy Stardust phase.

I sat next to her. 'Do you want to tell me what's going on, Ella?'

She turned to me and wiped a tear from her eye.

'It'll be okay. I've kicked him out.'

'Your husband?'

She squeezed the toy Ziggy Stardust and a fake human voice came out of it.

It's a godawful affair.

'Yes. No one needs to worry now. He won't be coming back.'

'Are you sure, Ella?'

She dropped Ziggy on the carpet and he squeaked. Then she grabbed my hands.

'You won't tell anyone, will you, Jen? If you do, they'll take Franny from me.'

Her fear rushed through me, her eyes glazed over. I pulled away from her and stood.

'What if he comes back and hurts you and Francine again, Ella?'

'He won't.' She took a mobile phone from her pocket. 'I'm going to ring a locksmith and get the locks changed.'

As she dialled the number, I glanced out of the window.

Abbey wasn't in the car.

Then I got a text.

I've gone to school with Francine.

I replied. *You better be telling the truth, Abs.*

Mum! I'll call you later.

'There, it's done. They're coming over now.'

She gazed at me like a puppy waiting to go for a walk. There was nothing else I could do there. So I put my arm on her shoulder.

'I'll come back when the kids have finished school, okay?'

Ella nodded.

I left as she picked Ziggy up.

I TOOK a detour on the way to the station, paying a visit to the social services building where Betty Green used to work. I told myself it was to speak to her former colleagues to see if they knew of Cole and any connection between Betty and him. Yet, deep down, I knew it wasn't the only reason I was there. If I just let it slip in the middle of a conversation and mentioned my concerns for an unnamed mother and daughter, I wouldn't be breaking my promise to Ella West. Would I?

The question ran around my mind as I spoke to the only two people in the office who were there when Green was.

'Betty was a hard worker,' they said, 'dedicated, but quiet.'

If something terrible happened to one of her clients, which I gathered was a frequent possibility, she took it personally.

'Working with children and families is always tricky,' one of Betty's former colleagues told me. 'The kids and sometimes the parents will try to justify abusive behaviour at home, which makes it much harder for us to uncover the truth. And sometimes, in that situation, the inevitable happens and there's a serious injury to deal with.'

As she spoke to me, as I watched her lips move, all I could think about was Francine and Ella. Wasn't it my responsibility to report what I'd seen? Yet, what of the promise I'd made to Ella West? If the husband was out of the picture, everything would return to normal, and there would be no risk of Francine being taken away.

And what would Abbey think if I said something to the social worker? Surely she'd believe I'd betrayed her friend?

Protection or betrayal?

My phone rang as I considered the question. It was Abbey. I apologised to the social worker and turned to leave, answering the call as I went.

'Are you okay, Abs? Is everything okay at school?'

'Yes, Mum. Don't panic. Can you pick Francine and me up after school? Her mum wants to cook us all a meal.'

'Of course, love.' Then I'd have a better chance to assess the situation. 'I'll see you in the usual spot.'

As I left the building, some worries evaporated from me. But not all of them.

Now I had to focus on finding a killer.

THE OTHERS HAD BEEN busy by the time I got to the office. The boxes retrieved from Cole's place had been organised by date, spanning twenty years of the former journalist's crime stories.

I told Jack about my trip to social services. He pointed at the files.

'Let's hope we have more luck with these.'

We split them between the four of us. I spent an hour reading about youth crime, drug trafficking, and prostitution, not finding one link to Betty Green or anything close to a clue to the identity of our killer. I was about to confer with the others when I received a summons from above.

Chief Superintendent Cassandra Cane, known behind her back as The Prophet because she had a reputation for stating the bleeding obvious every time she opened her mouth, had sent me an email. Considering how much she hated modern communication methods, I guessed she wasn't in a good mood. It was a terse one-line message requesting my presence in her office ASAP.

I told Jack where I was going. He pushed a pile of papers to the side.

'She probably wants an update on this case.' He narrowed his eyes. 'I've got nothing new to tell her; what about you?'

A shake of my head was the only reply I gave him. Sutton and Grealish buried their heads in old newspaper clippings as I left and made the short journey across the corridor. The Chief Super had recently moved her office to open-plan because, she'd said, it was the best way to present a welcoming presence to all her officers. All it did was make me wonder where she went for those conversations she kept from the rest of us.

She beckoned me to sit opposite her when I got there. There was fresh coffee and chocolate biscuits in front of her – with two cups and plates. As I peered at her face, trying to scrutinise what was behind those eyes, I felt as if I'd been invited to the Mad Hatter's tea party. Cane stood, came around the desk, picked up one cup and offered it to me.

'How are things at home, Jen? I hear Abbey is doing great with her music and the school football team.'

I took the drink and wondered who had been telling tales. Or perhaps Cane had been following me. Or following Abbey.

I grabbed a biscuit and bit it in half, tasting the chocolate as it crumbled down my throat. Then I sipped at the coffee before I replied.

'Everything's fine, Chief, but thanks for asking.'

I rolled a few crumbs between my teeth. Was I supposed to ask her how she was? I never got the chance.

'Well, that's good.' She put her drink down and placed both hands on her legs. 'I think that means this would be a perfect opportunity to talk about your promotion.'

I nearly dropped my cup and would have spat the rest of the biscuit all over her if I hadn't swallowed it.

'Promotion, ma'am?'

'Yes, Jen. You've been a DI for far too long and an excellent one, so it's about time you climbed up the next rung of the ladder.' She offered me another biscuit, which I took. 'How does Detective Chief Inspector Flowers sound?'

I thought about putting the whole biscuit into my mouth at once since it was open so wide.

'It sounds like I'd be getting a pay rise.'

Cane grinned at me. 'Indeed. About another five grand a year. Think about what you could do with that, Jen.'

I nibbled on the chocolate and thought about it a lot. Then we made some small talk for five minutes, and she never asked me about the case once. Finally, I told her I'd speak to Abbey about it – a promotion likely meant more work and more time away from home, if that was possible –

and get back to her. When I returned to the office, the others were sitting around the main table. They stopped talking as I entered.

'Are we in trouble, partner?'

My lips parted, ready to tell Jack what Cane had said, but the words didn't come. He'd never competed with me, but I wasn't sure how he'd take the news that I'd been offered a DCI position, and he hadn't.

I sat next to him. 'No, she only wanted an update.'

'And what did you tell her?' he said.

I looked between them all. 'Did you find anything useful in the boxes?'

All three of them shook their heads as Jack spoke.

'We've hit a brick wall, Jen.'

'That's what I told her.'

They stood and returned to their desks while I picked chocolate biscuit from my teeth.

27   PANDORA: THE BUS

After my parents died, I spent a long time living in different homes until I took my chances on the streets. But I soon discovered an alternative way of existing, one which allowed me to stay warm and away from most of the dangers which lurked inside London's shadows.

The buses which zigzagged across the city became my transitory houses, temporary communities of the lonely and the destitute. Having to rely on public transport, not having your own car places you at the lowest end of the social strata, but at least I had some control of where I stayed to keep dry and warm.

Wintertime was the worst. The wind would cut across my cheeks, dredging up memories of my parents and their deaths. So many times, I was the only one at the stop as the bus approached. The driver wouldn't acknowledge me as I got on, focused more on me having the right money for payment, scrutinising every scratch and line etched into my face.

I always tried to get my favourite spot at the rear, ignoring the upstairs noise and slumping into the seat.

Then, one time, something thumped on the floor above me, and a cocktail of laughter and obscenities drifted down. The top level was the most dangerous place on a bus, especially at night. My tattered gloves couldn't keep out the cold and I would always huddle as close to the back as I could, desperate to find the heat from the engine.

On this night, the bus pulled away as a heady aroma of the city seeped inside before the driver closed the door: fried chicken and onions mixed with cheap aftershave and perfume, alcohol fumes and petrol, making my stomach jump as we hit something. I glanced out the window, searching for what had gone under the wheels, but seeing nothing in the dark. On more than one occasion, I'd sat on a bus that had rolled over a dead body or hit some drunk staggering in the street.

Smoke assaulted my senses. I snapped my head up, convinced someone was smoking even though it was banned. We were drifting down the road, so it was easy to see the fire outside and a group of people standing around a burning flame nibbling at the frost surrounding it. I would be one of them later when there'd be nowhere left for me to huddle between stations.

A gaggle of drunks got on the bus at the next stop. They stank of alcohol, and I hoped they'd head upstairs. It was past midnight and too early for trouble. On the all-night buses, it usually happened around three in the morning when the clubs closed and the children of the night had nowhere left to go but home.

The gang shouted at each other and stumbled up to the top deck; those on the bottom breathed invisible sighs of relief. I looked across to the other side, trying to distract myself from what was happening above. A familiar face smiled at me. I didn't know her name or anything about her;

all I knew was she travelled on the buses like me, spending as much time as she could off the streets, finding warmth and a small degree of safety inside the transport. It was difficult to tell her age behind the dust and weariness swamping her. Her long hair was matted and clumped to her head, thick and dark; it could have been any colour underneath the dirt.

My smile cracked through my lips. I did my best to avoid my reflection in the window. If I didn't see how I looked, sometimes I could pretend to be the person I used to be, as I was before my parents died, and I disappeared inside the system. The drunks were singing; no trace of anger, only an expression of happiness. I couldn't remember the last time I'd felt like that. The smile I returned to the woman was of survival, of knowing we should be okay, at least for one more night.

It was safer and warmer there than on the street. Even in the summer, when the tourists flocked and their numbers increased, danger could spring from anywhere. More often than not, there was no warning, only the sudden thrust of a fist or a boot into the head, into the body. The body was preferable because the number of clothes I wore would cushion the blows. The face had no protection.

During the day, I'd spend my time wandering the streets, searching for something to eat or drink, often begging for money. Other times I'd visit the public libraries, not only for warmth, but for reading the books that were my only companions. I'd lose myself in the complete works of Shakespeare, Dickens, and Thomas Hardy. Sometimes I'd pick up old paperbacks for free, and when I couldn't sleep on the night buses, I'd use the time to flick through the pages and imagine I was Jack Reacher or Elizabeth Salander. I tried to be Harry Potter or Lyra Belacqua, but the reality of life around me wouldn't allow my brain to disappear into those realms of fantasy. It had been the opposite when I was a child. Then, I spent so much time in Oz and through the looking glass, I dreamt of living in another world.

And now I was.

When I wasn't on the bus or in the library, it was a case of finding somewhere to wash and get clean: a proper toilet was a bonus. Most of the public toilets in the city weren't free. Once darkness descended, or in the spring and summer no later than nine o'clock, I'd head for the station and the night buses. I soon discovered which were the best and the ones to avoid. The worst were the services along the routes which took in the most pubs and nightclubs. The drunks weren't always violent, but they could intimidate you in other ways: with verbal harassment and insults hurled at you because of the clothes you wore, the sound of your voice, or the colour of your skin.

Even now, when I see a bus passing by, or I travel on one, that time is still with me. When I found a proper place to live, I was twenty years old, leaving the buses behind me.

But there was a price to pay for that, one that I'm still paying.

28 JEN: THE FAMILY

I couldn't remember the last time I'd eaten at someone else's house. My stomach was already grumbling when I met Abbey and Francine outside the school. They were smiling and in a good mood. Francine still had her wrist protected with a bandage, but her eye appeared to be improving. I thought about bringing up the subject then, but Abbey's glare stopped that in its tracks. I left them to chat between themselves in the back of the car while I concentrated on getting there in one piece.

While they gossiped, I collected my thoughts regarding the murders of Green and Cole. Ten years ago, something had happened to them, but Green's former work colleagues and Cole's crime reporting files had provided nothing useful so far. Forensics hadn't discovered anything to connect the killer or killers, and we had no eyewitnesses to the crimes or CCTV footage to go on. So we were no further forward than when we'd started.

There was the vague description Betty Green's ex-husband had given us, but that had led nowhere. It was the same with Cole's Facebook page and the Betty Green who'd liked one of his comments.

Yet Chief Superintendent Cane had offered me a promotion.

I assumed it was because of my work over the last fifteen years.

But I didn't have to accept it. It wouldn't look good to my superiors, especially Cane, but the idea of becoming a DCI wasn't filling me with joy – I'd spend even less time with Abbey and would put Jack's nose out of joint, not that he'd complain.

Francine removed keys from her pocket as we arrived at the West house. I wondered if I should mention her mother had changed the locks. But, I didn't need to as Ella West opened the door to greet us. She looked different from this morning, younger, and happier. After kicking her abusive husband out of the house, I guess she would be.

But how would Francine take the news?

The girls ignored Ella and went straight inside. It didn't appear to bother Ella as she stepped towards me and threw her arms around my shoulders. She squeezed me for an uncomfortable five seconds before letting go.

'I'm so happy you could come, Jen.' She pushed her face so close to mine, I could smell the lavender of her perfume. 'And thank you for not saying anything about..., well, you know, what happened this morning.'

Fresh makeup hid the mark on her cheek.

'That's okay, Ella. I'm looking forward to the food.'

She kept on grinning as she led me into the house. The aroma of pasta and bolognese warmed my heart.

'I'm glad, Jen. I know you're driving, but I hope you can have one glass of wine.'

At least one. 'Of course, Ella.'

We went into the living room, where I saw that the broken mirror was gone and a framed print of the poster for *Metropolis* covered the spot on the wall. The table at the back was set up for dining.

'Pour drinks for you and me, Jen, and I'll see what the girls want.'

She went to leave, but I grabbed her arm before she could.

'Do you want to talk about your husband with Francine here?'

I wasn't keen to get Abbey involved, but she had to know what was happening to her best friend if she didn't already.

The colour drained from Ella's face.

'It's all sorted, Jen. He's gone and won't be coming back.' Determination seeped out of her eyes. 'I can promise you that.'

'How do you know, Ella?'

'Because I told him you knew everything, and if he returned, you'd arrest him.'

I was contemplating how to reply to that when the girls burst into the room.

'Mum, Francine and me have been writing songs all day. We've got enough new stuff for an album. Would you like to hear them?'

Ella took that as a hint to pour the wine as I answered.

'Haven't the two of you been at school?'

Francine slumped into the sofa. 'Thursday is a dull day, Ms Flowers, nothing but geography and French and they're no good to anyone. Unless you want to live in France, and we don't.'

Abbey sat next to her. 'So we had loads of free time to write the important stuff.'

Francine giggled. 'They might be a bit too modern for you, though, Ms Flowers.'

The girls laughed together as I stared at Francine, who hadn't looked at her mother since she'd got home.

Did she know her father wasn't coming back? And if she did, how did she feel about it?

Ella handed me a glass of wine. 'What do you want to drink, girls?'

Francine jumped from the sofa. 'I'll get some Cokes.'

I sat next to my daughter as Ella followed hers into the kitchen. I took one sip of my drink and turned to Abbey.

'Francine didn't fall down the stairs, did she?' She didn't reply. 'I know what happened to her eye and her wrist. And I know what happened to Mrs West.'

She stared at her legs as she spoke. 'Mrs West?'

'Yes, Ella West. I know her husband hit her, just like he did to Francine.'

'Oh.'

'Why didn't you tell me what was going on?'

'Dinner is ready.'

Ella returned, carrying a tray with pasta bowls and bolognese. Abbey jumped from the sofa, sitting next to Francine at the table. I took my drink and joined them.

There was no talk about the missing Mr West or what he'd done to his family, no mention of their bruises and what had happened in the house this morning. Instead, the conversation started with the girls' music and how they'd be famous internet stars. Then it went to the football team and how well Abbey was doing. We'd finished the main course and were starting on apple pie and ice cream for dessert when Ella threw me with a surprising comment.

'Abbey tells me she met her grandmother the other day for the first time.'

I'd had the last of my wine fifteen minutes ago, but as I peered at Ella, my stomach called out for another. I glanced at Abbey, who was whispering to Francine.

I reached for the empty glass before pulling my hand back.

'Yes, my mother has been ill for a while, so things have been difficult.'

Ella's face darkened. 'My mum had dementia for five years before she died.' Her eyes appeared as tiny pinpricks on her face as she spoke. 'She lived here with us, and I gave up work to look after her. I couldn't bear to put her in one of those homes. You hear so many horrible things about them.'

I couldn't tell if she was empathising with me or being critical.

'Can we go to the garage and rehearse, Mum?' Abbey said.

It wasn't my house, so I didn't know how to reply. I thought Francine might say something to her mother, but she didn't.

'Go on, girls, just keep the noise down while Jen and I are chatting,' Ella said.

They didn't need a second invitation to leave. It was six o'clock, and if they were playing music, I knew I'd be stuck for at least another hour. I studied Ella's grin and wished I'd left the car at home.

Then she poured me another glass of wine, and I didn't stop her. The drive back wasn't far and two glasses wouldn't affect me that much.

I took the drink when she finished and raised it to her.

'Thanks.'

'It's nothing, Jen. I'm glad we got to meet face to face.'

She glanced towards the door. 'Even if it was in unusual circumstances.' She drank her wine. 'And I'm happy Franny is friends with Abbey. She's always found it difficult making friends, even from primary school, because of her condition.' I assumed she was talking about her daughter's alopecia. 'And playing in a band has boosted her confidence. Then she got to play in the school team, and she's like a different girl to what she was a year ago.' She stood and came around the table, glass in one hand while she put the other on my arm. 'I can't thank you enough for what your family has done for us.'

'Think nothing of it, Ella.' I glanced at the sofa. 'Shall we make ourselves comfortable while the girls are away?'

She nodded as the noise of electronic keyboards sounding like an ice-cream van on acid drifted out of the garage and into the living room.

We sat opposite each other and sipped our drinks. Was I going to take her word that the unnamed husband wouldn't return? It seemed I had no choice unless I wanted to risk having Francine being taken from Ella. But it still worried me. I'd witnessed the terrible consequences of abusive partners returning to their family homes.

Did I want to take that risk?

It was just one more dilemma I didn't need.

'How did Abbey get on with her grandmother?' And this was another one. 'I guess it can't have been easy for her, or you, what with your mother's condition.'

'She can visit her when she wants, but it's difficult for me at the moment because of work.'

Her eyes lit up. 'Are you involved in finding the killer of those two people who were burnt to death?'

Had Abbey mentioned what I was working on to Francine and her mother?

'I can't talk about ongoing investigations, Ella.'

'Oh yes, of course, Jen, I didn't mean to pry. I'm sorry.'

I changed the subject.

'What was it like having your mother living with you?'

Her shoulders slumped into the sofa.

'It was difficult, but she was my mum, and you have to look after your family, don't you?'

'How did your husband take it?'

Her face darkened. 'Ben tried his best, but, well, he and my mother had never got on, and when she was diagnosed with dementia, it only made things worse. But he knew how important it was for me.' She cradled the glass in her hands. 'It must have been difficult bringing Abbey up on your own.'

My daughter's voice came screeching out of the garage, singing something about monstrous spiders and gene manipulation.

'We've done okay.' I stared straight into her eyes. 'What will you tell Francine about her father?'

She didn't flinch from my gaze. 'I'll tell her the truth. I don't think it's good to lie to children, do you?'

'No, Ella, I don't.' I just keep certain things from mine. 'If you need any help, here's my mobile number.' The one I only used for work.

I wrote it on a piece of paper and passed it to her. She smiled as she took it.

'I will, Jen. But don't worry about us. We'll be fine.' Then, a loud wailing like strangled cats being cooked in a microwave vibrated through the room. 'Well, apart from that noise.'

We laughed together and I finished my drink. 'I think I should have a coffee before I take Abbey home.'

Ella nodded. 'Of course.' She stood. 'I'll get you one.'

I watched her leave and listened to the sounds masquerading as music screeching out of the garage. I hoped both Francine and Abbey would be okay in the coming months as they continued to murder their instruments.

Then my mind drifted to two other murders.

29 PANDORA: THE NOISE

I took the Tube to Tottenham White Hart Lane station. My earphones were glued to my head; I was listening to music and trying not to remember one of my many disastrous relationships, but it was hard since a former boyfriend was a Spurs fan. The only way I could get away from him was by pretending to be in love with Thierry Henry.

The Tube stank of sweat and cheap perfume as the bloke sitting opposite me started singing some horrible tune from *Cats* or *Les Misérables*. Everyone in the crowded carriage turned their heads from him while I had to increase the volume on my phone, letting Prince relax me with harrowing tales of his childhood dressed up as 1980s funk-pop. My Murder Diary was close to my chest, providing comfort on what I hoped would be my penultimate trip on this journey of death and revenge.

Finding where Wallace lived had been easy enough. However, I didn't want to leave any electronic traces or use paid websites, so I used a different method. A quick browse online led me to his social media and, in particular, his

Twitter account. He enjoyed taking moody black and white photos of the capital, sometimes posting hints of his location. Two days ago, he posted a picture of the skyline where he lived, including the rooftops and a pub on the corner. Then it was a case of using Google Earth to trace the pub and the houses nearby. I matched that with other posts he'd made of the area and pinpointed the place where he got the view from. Then I rang the local council and said I worked for a credit card company trying to locate a bad debtor.

Anyone with half a brain would have said no or asked for credentials, but the dozy mare on the other end of the phone believed my lies hook, line and sinker. After two minutes of speaking to her, not only did I have Wallace's address, but a rambling account of how many times his neighbours had complained about him. He liked to develop his photographs at home and the place stank of chemicals most of the time.

Chemicals. How handy would they be once I set him on fire?

But that was for later once he'd told me the truth. And he had to do that. He was the last link in the chain, the final part of the jigsaw. If he couldn't give me what I needed, there was nowhere else for me to go.

And that didn't bear thinking about.

Most of the street contained blocks of flats, and I guessed he'd taken most of his high-rise photos from their rooftops. His place was one of the few remaining houses, built in the early days of the twentieth century. I strode past a cemetery to get there, amused that soon, his neighbours would have nothing to complain about.

I'd checked everything I could about him and the house before heading out, making sure there would be no surprises to trip me up when I got there. If he had a dog, for example, it might prove problematic. But, through my research, I discovered he was only an old man living on his own, seeing out his days taking black and white photographs of the city he'd betrayed.

The streetlights flickered as I went, helping me embrace the cover of darkness while complementing the scarf and jacket pulled up to my face. I didn't expect any working CCTV in the area, but you never could tell when someone might stride by with their phone, taking videos or photos. Modern technology had made things much more difficult for the jobbing criminal.

I slipped down the gap between Wallace's house and the neighbour's, catching a whiff of unemptied rubbish bins and hearing the whine of something electrical in the air. I snapped my head up, worried it might be a drone and thankful it was only an over-excited telephone line.

By the time I reached the back door, I had the tools in my hand to get inside – my long stretch in prison hadn't been a waste.

I fiddled with the lock for twenty seconds before it sprang open. The wind whistled behind me as I entered the kitchen, moving silently into the house. It smelt of fried onions and overcooked sausages. Grease stuck to my shoes as I inched into the corridor and stared at the entrance to my left. I stepped past a garish lamp covered in pictures of small dogs and peered through the gap in the doorway. All I could see was a cramped bookcase, but the TV's noise seeped from the room, all loud explosions and people swearing: I assumed he was watching *Question Time* on the BBC as I pushed my way inside.

'I wondered when you'd get here.'

Wallace sat slumped in an armchair in the corner, his feet surrounded by empty beer cans and crushed pizza boxes. He didn't appear surprised to see me, which I found curious, but not unsettling. It gladdened my heart to know he'd been waiting all this time for his punishment to arrive.

I smiled at him.

'You can wonder no more.'

He used the TV remote to increase the sound to ear-shattering levels.

'I don't want the neighbours to know what's going on here.'

Perhaps he thought I was some prostitute he'd hired. If so, what a disappointment he was in for.

'Won't they complain about the noise?'

He finished a can of beer and dropped it into the mass on the floor.

'Nah; they know I'm deaf in one ear.' He tapped the side of his head. 'All those times listening to scumbags shouting at me has done my hearing in something rotten. I feel like I was the drummer in a heavy metal band for the last thirty years.'

'Do you understand why I'm here?'

'Of course. Once I saw what happened to the social worker and that bent journo, I knew you'd come for me.'

The laughter slipped out of me. 'That's rich, you calling him dishonest, don't you think?'

'That's different. I did what I had to do to protect people; he was only in it for the money. Same as Green. They didn't care about those kids.'

My heart thumped against my chest like a jackhammer.

'And you did?'

Wallace reached down to grab another beer. He swigged half of it before he replied, with the booze trickling over his cracked lips.

'I tried my best.' He waved the can towards me. 'But one man can't fight against an army.'

I moved closer to the TV to get a better look at him, suspicious he might have a weapon down the side of the sofa.

'What do you mean by that?'

'People like me and you are ineffectual against power and influence.'

'You took money to keep your mouth shut.'

'I'm not proud of it, but that wasn't the main reason. They threatened my family, said they'd kill my sister and give her kids to a bunch of wealthy perverts. There was nothing I could do.'

'But you know who they are.'

He dropped the beer and shook his head.

'I can't tell you. It doesn't matter about me now; the cancer in my gut will finish me soon enough. But I have to protect my family.'

I knew all about protecting family and who I'd failed in that duty. But, peering into his face, peeling away the fear and determination in his eyes, I recognised he'd never tell me what I wanted.

But I tried.

'Just give me a name, Wallace. Then I'll deal with them, and they won't be able to hurt your family or anybody else's.'

He leant towards me, drowning me in whisky fumes.

'It doesn't matter that you can kill the likes of me and the other two; we're nobodies in the grand scheme of things. Those you're after are different; nothing ever sticks to them no matter what good people try to do.'

I thought about torturing him, but I didn't have the stomach for it.

And from looking into his dead eyes, I knew it would make no difference.

Empty cans scattered as I kicked them away and moved towards him, my hand already inside my jacket for what I needed. Of course, he'd give me nothing, but his punishment was unavoidable.

30 JEN: THE BASEMENT

It was three in the morning when I got the call, my hand fumbling for the mobile as the cat jumped from the foot of my bed. It scampered from the room as I answered the phone.

'I hope this is to tell me you're eloping with Tiffany, Jack.'

'Our killer has struck again.'

I rubbed at my face in an attempt to squeeze my brain awake.

'Now?'

'No, it was four hours ago. The Fire and Rescue Service has finished at the scene and it's safe to enter. Forensics and Scene of Crime Officers have also swept the house.'

My blurry eyes peered at the digital clock beaming at me.

'So this can wait until morning?'

It already was Friday morning, but it still felt like the night to me.

'It could.' He sounded wide awake. 'But considering

who the victim is, I thought you might want to get a head start while the scene is still fresh.'

I swung my legs out of bed and got dressed as I asked the question.

'It's someone important?'

'That's not for me to say. The victim is Ged Wallace, aged sixty-six.'

I was in the bathroom, staring at my bleary-eyed face when I spoke.

'Am I supposed to know that name?'

'Maybe, maybe not. Wallace retired in 2010 after a four-decade career as a copper in the Metropolitan Police Force.'

I dropped my toothbrush into the washbasin, the red and blue paste dripping over my lips.

'Shit!'

'Did you know Wallace?'

I wiped my mouth clean. 'Never heard of him, but this can't be good.'

'It isn't for him.'

I spat into the bowl and returned to the bedroom, leaving Jack on the speaker as I finished dressing.

'Did the professionals find anything useful?'

His sigh was loud down the phone. 'Not from what I've seen in the initial reports.' A female voice in the background called for him. 'Shall I text you the address?'

'It sounds like you're busy, partner. So I'll go on my own.'

I was downstairs with the car keys in my free hand.

'We do this together, Jen. Either now or in six hours. It's your choice.'

I'd already made my decision. 'Come and pick me up.'

Which he did. Forty minutes after the call had woken

me up, we were standing in the street staring at the outside of Wallace's house, which looked like it was untouched. A cemetery was on the left. The streetlights flickered on and off in front of it, so it resembled a scene from *The Exorcist*. There wasn't another soul anywhere, only a chill wind biting at my throat.

I should have told Abbey where I was going.

Jack had the house keys in his hand.

'The Fire Investigation Officer, Greenham, spoke to me on the phone before I called you. He confirmed it was like the other two crime scenes, with only localised fire damage in one room.'

We strode up the path. 'We have a conscientious killer to catch.'

He nodded as he unlocked the door. 'That's something to be thankful for.'

The smell hit me as I stepped into the corridor, that familiar aroma of burnt wood and human flesh. I peered at a lamp covered in illustrations of small dogs.

'I assume they've removed Wallace's remains?'

'They have. I'll text you the photos and video Greenham sent me.'

We stood outside the living room. 'Just show me your phone for now.'

He handed it to me and we stepped through the door. I looked at the images on the screen as he took two torches from his jacket and gave me one.

'The Fire and Rescue Service turned off the power for safety reasons.'

He shone his light at the spot where Wallace must have died. I glanced from the scorched furniture to the photo on the phone, scrutinising the image of Wallace's burnt remains in the chair. I peered at the armrest and noticed a dark outline of a hand, all that remained of Ged Wallace's sixty-six years on this planet.

Around the bottom of the sofa were piles of ashes with bits of pizza boxes and melted beer cans sticking out of the debris. I moved from the chair and studied the rest of the room, getting an idea of the layout, which was always difficult to assess from photos and even videos. The TV was untouched, but a thin film of ash clung to most walls, hiding the flowered wallpaper behind its dark veneer.

I took a deep breath and tasted the smoke which continued to linger in the air.

'We should check the rest of the house, Jack.'

'Sure, partner.' He gazed at his phone. 'The SOCOs have checked all the rooms upstairs and downstairs. But, unfortunately, they didn't have time to examine a shed in the garden and the basement. So they're coming back in the morning for those.'

The light from my torch dimmed without me touching anything, so I smacked one hand against it until it flickered into life.

'Lucky them. We'll get this done quicker if we split up. Which do you prefer?'

He walked towards the back. 'You know how much I love gardening.'

'Text me if you find something interesting.'

The basement door was on my left and unlocked. Jack was whistling *Light My Fire* as I opened it and pointed the torch at the steps. The wood creaked along with the bones in my legs as I went down. The shadows bounced through the torchlight as I swept it from side to side, breathing in a musty aroma of damp and engine oil. The illumination danced off the shelves pushed against the walls, each of them crammed with yellowing newspapers and magazines.

They were a fire hazard in themselves and I was thankful the blaze from the living room hadn't made it this far.

But why hadn't our killer torched the whole building and done the same with the other two crime scenes? That would have been the perfect way of covering up any evidence they'd left behind.

Not that we'd found any so far. Perhaps this place would be different.

I stepped onto the wooded floor and moved towards the closest set of shelves, fanning the torch over the stack of magazines, hoping there might be something there to illuminate our investigation. Instead, I inched back in disappointment on discovering they were only fishing publications.

The gloom encircled me as I laughed, picturing myself as a desperate angler throwing hooks into the water and coming up with nothing.

I tempered my frustration as I turned and noticed where someone had ripped up the floorboards. Splinters and bits of wood lay over the floor as I knelt and shone the torch into the gap. It was big enough to hold a large box or a ring binder, but it looked empty. I was about to reach inside when I saw flickering light a few feet from me.

A woman moved forward, a bright red scarf covering the lower half of her face, a long burning match in one hand, a tattered notebook in the other.

'Don't move or speak, and I won't set you on fire.'

I ignored the threat. 'I'm not covered in petrol.'

'But the surrounding ground is.'

I stared at the wood, smelt the aroma of rotten eggs at my feet before returning my attention to the flickering flame across from me.

'Is that why you killed Wallace and the others, for his police notebook?'

Pinpricks of light shone in her eyes as she waved the book at me.

'You mean this, the notebook which records the secrets he kept buried and hidden away? And do you know why he did that, your fellow officer?'

The floor creaked above me before I could reply.

'Are you okay down there, Jen? I thought I heard a strange noise.'

I didn't take my eyes off the woman, her expression telling me what would happen if I said the wrong thing to my partner.

'There's nothing here, Jack. You check the back garden and I'll meet you outside.'

'Will do.' His footsteps drifted away as the woman moved to the stairs.

'You made the right choice.'

'What will you do now?'

The flame continued to flicker in her hand. 'I'm guessing I'll find what I need inside this book.'

'And that's something you've killed three people for?'

She was in the middle of the stairs when she replied. 'I'd burn this entire world down to get to the person who took my daughter from me.'

That's when it hit me.

'I know why you didn't burn down their homes.'

The flame appeared to be taking an age to reach the bottom of the match.

'Please, enlighten me.'

'You've been looking for something all this time, and you didn't find it with Green or Cole.' I pointed at the notebook. 'And now you've got it with Wallace's notes, which, I guess, is why you killed him and the others.'

'You'll never know, copper.'

I calculated how quickly I could get up the stairs once she stepped into the corridor, but it was a fruitless exercise as she threw the match towards me. She was through the door as I grabbed for my flying death, my fingers clutching at it, but not connecting. It landed at my feet and rolled into the corner as I waited for the petrol to light. Images of Abbey flew through my head, of all the things we'd done together and of everything I'd miss. I thought of my mother and the possible early onset of dementia I wouldn't have to worry about anymore.

My eyes closed against my will as I lay in the damp, the stink of petrol sticking to me like a lead overcoat. Then I heard Abbey's voice in my head telling me to get up.

So I did.

My breath was stuck in my chest when I realised the flame had flickered out before it had hit the ground. Energy returned to me as I pushed my hands into the wet floor and stood. Then I sprinted up the stairs and out of the basement. The woman was gone. I ran into the garden and saw the body sprawled near the rose bushes.

I was calling for the ambulance as I rushed forward.

———

THE PARAMEDICS ARRIVED JUST as Jack came round and rubbed at the bruise growing on the back of his neck. Once I knew he was okay, I left him with them and returned to the Wallace basement. The ruptured floor-boards were easy to spot, the broken parts sticking up in the far corner. I wasn't sure how she'd done it since I couldn't see what she'd used; unless it was her fingers, which would be perfect as it would have left DNA. I slipped the protective gloves on and hoped the forensic team would find something useful.

A creature scuttled inside the gap when I put my hand into it, hairy legs running over my skin as I searched for anything she'd left behind. Finally, I touched something plastic in the corner of the gap. It was right on the tip of my covered fingers, yet out of my reach. Footsteps trundled down the stairs behind me as I forced my knee into the wood and extended my arm so far, it felt like I was fixed on a medieval torture rack.

'What happened in here, Jen?'

Jack's voice was strained, the words crawling over his lips. I reached as far as possible and pulled the plastic towards me. I dragged it out of the dark and rolled on to my back, staring at my partner. He helped me up.

'Some woman cracked up this floor and removed Wallace's police notebook. Then she threatened to set me on fire if I didn't let her leave.'

He let go of my hand and glanced at the petrol stain behind him.

'I wondered what that smell was.' He touched the nape of his neck. 'I guess she's the one who hit me as well.'

'Did you see her?'

'Only fleetingly as I crashed into the garden; about your height, short dark hair and piercing blue eyes. Do you know her?'

I shook my head. 'I don't think so. Maybe she's someone I arrested years ago, but the memory isn't coming back to me.'

'Do you believe Wallace's police notebook contains details of his investigations?'

'Whatever it is, it's important to her.'

'Important enough to kill for.' He pointed at the bag in my hand. 'What's in there?'

I released the zip and removed the contents: four credit cards for different banks.

'They all have variations of his name on them: Ted Wallace, Fred Wallace, Freddy Wallace, and Ed Wallace.'

'He had a vivid imagination.' Jack scrutinised them without touching the plastic. 'It seems like our former fellow officer had quite a few secrets.'

I replaced the contents into the bag.

'Let's return to the station and see what we can get from them.'

I followed him up the steps, glancing back only once to the spot where I'd nearly gone up in flames.

31 PANDORA: THE FRIEND

The cold embraced me as I slipped away from Wallace's house and hid inside the shadows. My heart was fit to burst as I felt the copper's notebook pushed up against my ribs, adrenalin flowing through me so much I couldn't go home.

Spots of rain dropped over my hands as I removed the phone from my jacket. There were three unread texts from Gladys. I scanned them while ensuring nobody else was on the street. It was 5 am, so I didn't expect anyone to be around, but you never knew in London.

Gladys's messages were short but desperate, asking to see me about something important. A week ago, I'd have brushed her off, ignored the texts and focused on myself. But after the parties, I'd grown attached to her. I hadn't had what you'd call a real friend in an age, not since my schooldays. A ten-year stint in prison forces you into close relationships you wouldn't have had on the outside. But, even if you become friends with somebody, you can't continue with it after prison because the probation service doesn't want you to fraternise with former prisoners. It's a curious thing, considering there were two women inside at the same time as me who got married while forced to endure the government's hospitality. I guessed they didn't have to live apart once released, but nothing would surprise me.

My mind was wandering and I was unsure why. I should have been heading home for two excellent reasons: first, to get off the street in case the police pulled me over and started asking awkward questions. Second, I had to find somewhere private to read Wallace's notebook.

As I sheltered in a doorway, the rain became heavier and I stared at the book. My place was a forty-minute walk in one direction, while Gladys's flat was ten minutes in the other. I considered what route to take as I thought about my encounters with those coppers in Wallace's house. I'd only gone a few hundred yards from his home after killing him when his last words meant something to me.

'It's hard to bury our secrets, but we have to try,' was what he'd said before going up in flames.

He didn't scream, only sitting in that chair as the fire consumed him. I'd watched him burn like a candle before I left, kicking myself again for coming away empty-handed and knowing there was nowhere else for me to look in search of what I'd lost.

It was only as the smoke drifted out of the house that I understood what he'd meant: he'd buried his secrets in that house somewhere. I ran back as fast as I could, glancing at the garden, but not picturing Wallace as a horticulturist. Instead, I rushed downstairs as the sirens approached.

When I stumbled into the gloom, I knew I faced a dilemma: leave again and pray the police didn't discover what I was after or wait in the basement in the hope the fire service wouldn't find me there. I was sure the coppers wouldn't be allowed into the building until it had been made safe, and that would be in the morning.

So I took the risk, hiding behind some well-stacked shelves when the fire officers completed a cursory look into the basement. Then I heard the forensic people going about their business upstairs as I waited for them all to leave.

Once they did, it didn't take long to find the loose floor-boards and get them up. Then I had Wallace's notebook in my hand when the detectives entered the building. Thankfully, they split up once inside. I'm not sure I could have dealt with both of them at once. As it was, the woman proved trickier than I thought she'd be.

But I got away and they were no closer to identifying me. So I couldn't waste any time with anything else – I had to read what was in Wallace's notebook, hoping he'd recorded his involvement in the crimes.

Yet still, I didn't move from that spot, no matter how drenched I was.

And I knew why I was reluctant to get inside and open the book.

Fear of disappointment had taken root in every part of me, turning my flesh into ice and melting my brain so I couldn't think straight.

I zipped my jacket as far as it would go up to my throat, tasting rainwater as I stepped out of the shadows and headed in the opposite direction to my flat. I needed to talk to someone, anyone, about anything, so it might as well be Gladys in her hour of need.

The weather attacked my head as I marched down the pavement, hunched over, pushing the water from my mobile as I checked the GPS directions. Ten minutes later, I was outside Gladys's place and texting her. She was at the door before I could put the phone back in my pocket.

'Come in, Pandora, and get dry.'

She dragged me inside, my body now ready to drop and my brain a dollop of mashed potato. I stood in the corridor as she took my jacket and hung it up. Then she went into another room and returned with a large towel.

'Thanks,' I said as I grabbed it from her and dried my head.

'Would you like a hot drink or maybe something stronger?' she said.

I squeezed the damp from my hair and felt the temptation for alcohol growing in me. But I knew it would be a mistake.

'A peppermint tea will do if you have one, Gladys.'

She nodded. 'Of course. You go in the living room and sit next to the heater while I make the drinks.'

I stepped into the room as I continued to run the towel through my hair. At least Wallace's book was dry inside my jacket. My legs gave way as I slumped into a chair near a blazing hot radiator. I heard Gladys whistling in the kitchen as I glanced around the room. All the windows were boarded up, and the walls were covered in pages from old comic books: panels from pre-code horror comics featuring gashed eyeballs, split torsos, and skulls crushed with axes mixed with 50s sci-fi bug-eyed monsters and women in barely-there costumes which were most inappropriate for space travel. The floor was missing a carpet, with a sofa but no TV, stereo, or computer. Instead, half a dozen tattered paperbacks lay on a table in the middle of the room.

Gladys returned with the drinks and a plate of biscuits. Something clawed at the insides of my guts and I couldn't remember the last time I'd eaten. So I grabbed a biscuit and ate it in two quick bites.

'Thanks,' I said as bits of chocolate trickled over my lips.

'It's my pleasure, Pandora, but I'm feeling guilty now.'

She sat on the sofa opposite me, pulling her legs up underneath her as if she was a teenager. I sipped on the hot drink, burning the insides of my mouth as an image of Wallace in flames flashed through my mind.

'Why do you feel guilty?' I was already warming up, but the heater also added to my sleepiness.

'Oh, you know, for sending those daft texts and getting you out at night in such terrible weather.'

I shook my head, about to say not to worry because I was out anyway, before realising how strange that would have sounded.

'Forget about it, Gladys.' I put the tea on the floor next to me. 'Why don't you tell me what's wrong?'

She narrowed her eyes and looked sheepish.

'It's about the engagement. I'm wondering if I've been too hasty. I mean, I hardly know him.'

Because she hadn't mentioned his name, I didn't either.

'Just because you're engaged, it doesn't mean you have to get married soon, or at all. Take your time to get to know each other.'

Gladys beamed at me. 'Oh, I knew you'd be sensible about this, Pandora. That's what everybody says about you at the office.'

I glanced at the rain drying on me, never having realised people had been talking about me at all. Or that they might have liked me. I gazed deep into her eyes.

'Life is all about being washed up again and again, trying to find another track, another path to the future. Then getting washed up again. And then continuing. There aren't that many straight lines for anyone, Gladys. All we can do is get up in the morning and be the best version of ourselves.'

She reached over and patted me on the hand.

'You sound like you've been through a lot, Pandora.'

I smiled at her. 'Please, call me Pan.'

She gripped my fingers. 'Thank you for being my friend, Pan.'

A real friend, something lost to me for so many years. I'd had a good friend ages ago at school. We'd been more than friends, she and I, but I got scared and ran into the arms of the wrong man at the wrong time. I gazed at Gladys's unusual wallpaper and wondered what my life would have been like if I'd never met him. Better in many ways, but then I wouldn't have had the most precious thing in my life: Catherine, my daughter.

The thought of what happened pressed on my heart and I felt the copper's notebook against my chest. Now I wanted to grab it, turn those pages, expose its secrets with my new friend, and share my pain with another human being.

Of course, I didn't because that would have meant telling her the terrible things I'd done. And they were awful, even though I knew they were justified.

But I couldn't place that burden on her.

So I didn't. I sat there for two hours, letting her talk, listening to the doubts she had and trying my best to reassure her.

Then Gladys rang for a taxi to take me home. I was all dried out and ready for what was in the book next to my heart.

I handed the credit cards to Constable Grealish at the station and asked her to discover what she could about them. Jack continued to claw at the back of his neck.

'Perhaps you should go home, partner.'

He shook his head which, from his grimace, only appeared to make things worse.

'No. I feel we're near to the end of this now. You look like you need a rest; you got little sleep last night.'

'I'm okay, and you're right about us getting close to ending this. The woman was desperate to return to the crime scene and show herself like that. Wallace's notebook was important to her, our killer, so I'm assuming they knew each other. Let's check his case files.'

Jack went to his computer, and I sat in front of mine. At least with modern technology, we didn't have to trawl through reams of paperwork. Wallace had joined the force in 1970, so most of his reports would be recorded as digital documents, and we had a handy system that organised them all.

Criminal records information is held on two central

systems: the Police National Computer (PNC) records convictions, cautions, reprimands, warnings and arrests. In addition, the Police National Database (PND) records "soft" local police intelligence, for example, details of investigations that did not lead to any further action.

Ged Wallace had case files on both systems, so we split into two teams: Jack and Constable Grealish worked through the records on the PNC, while Sutton and I trawled through the PND. For a man with a forty-year career in the Met, it was a lot of reading; I was peering into a computer screen until my head throbbed. It was a full day's session, with only lunch and visits to the toilet breaking up the work. By the time we reached five o'clock, the consensus between all of us was it had been a waste.

Jack scrubbed at the stubble on his chin.

'More than a hundred files and not one mention of Green or Cole; not even a single line about social services or any journalists he might have known.'

I sipped at cold coffee and grimaced.

'I still feel we're missing something right in front of us.' I looked at Constable Sutton. 'Sarah, is there a way we can link the files on the PNC and the PND together or side by side as a comparison?'

'I'm not sure, ma'am, but I don't see why not. What we've been reading is only a bunch of databases, so I should be able to create relationships between them.'

Jack sighed. 'Don't mention relationships to me.'

I grinned at him. 'Things not going well with you and Tiffany?'

'You tell me, Jen. Tiff wants to have a baby.'

Sutton and Grealish stopped typing and glanced at us.

'Wow.' I didn't know what else to say.

'That was my reaction.' The constables returned to their

work as he leant closer to me. 'I mean, I'll be thirty-eight on my next birthday. Isn't that too old to be a father?'

Before I could even think of an appropriate reply, Grealish piped up.

'My dad was forty when I was born, sir.'

He peered at her as if she'd answered all of his problems. Before the conversation developed further, Sutton informed us she'd finished her task.

'I've placed the report in the shared drive on the network, ma'am. Let me know if you require any other modifications to the data.'

I returned to my desk and scanned through her work. I stared at it for five minutes before something struck me. Sutton had combined the PNC and the PND reports and laid them out in date order, from Wallace's first report in 1970 to his last, forty years later. There weren't many at the beginning, but they'd increased over time as he progressed through the force and climbed up the promotional ladder.

My back creaked as I pushed into the chair and moved from the computer.

'Does anyone else see the glaring omission that I do?'

Jack rubbed at his eyes. 'My head hurts, Jen, so put me out of my misery.'

I got up and went to his desk.

'Wallace was a busy copper, filing regular reports weekly for most of his police career.' I leant over Jack's shoulder and pointed at his screen. 'Apart from here, June to September in 2010. There's nothing for those four months.'

Jack narrowed his eyes and stared at the monitor.

'Maybe he was on holiday.'

I looked at Sutton. 'Can you check, Sarah?'

She did just that, finding Wallace's record listing all holiday and sickness periods.

'Wallace's holidays in 2010 were one week in February, two in May, and three in October, ma'am. And he didn't take any sick leave that year.'

I sat in the empty seat next to Jack. 'So what was he doing between June and September 2010?'

'He retired in December 2010, so perhaps he was just winding down after forty years of plodding through London's streets,' Jack said.

I pushed my chair closer to his computer and grabbed the mouse.

'Don't mind me, partner.'

He stood. 'Be my guest, Jen. I'll get fresh coffee.'

Jack left the office for the drinks while I went through Wallace's files again for 2010. It didn't take long to find what I wanted. By the time Jack had returned with drinks for all of us, I knew where I'd be going next; and it wasn't far away.

He handed me a mug. 'Did you discover anything useful?'

I twisted the computer towards him as he sat. 'I believe so. The person who would best know what Wallace was doing in those months would be the Senior Investigation Officer on his other cases that year, don't you think?'

'It makes sense to me.'

I pointed at the screen. 'How about that, then?'

He lifted the drink to his mouth, but stopped short of planting the mug on his lips and let out a long whistle.

'The Prophet.'

Indeed. Chief Superintendent Cassandra Cane or, as she was ten years ago, SIO Cane. Our boss might have the answers we needed to solve this case.

'Sarah, will you see if the Chief Super is in her office?'

Sutton got up and nodded. 'Yes, ma'am.'

Jack swivelled in his chair. 'Do you think she'll remember Wallace after all this time?'

I laughed. 'Come on, Jack. You know how good her memory is.'

He shook his head. 'Well, she does like to remind me of any minor mistake I made years ago, so yeah, I know what you mean.'

Constable Sutton returned two minutes later.

'Chief Superintendent Cane is in her office, ma'am.'

'Thanks, Sarah.' I looked at Jack. 'Are you coming with me?'

He grinned at me. 'Why not? It's not like we're going anywhere else with this, are we?'

I left my coffee on the desk and followed him, taking the short walk to The Prophet's office. He knocked on her door and we entered without being asked. The Chief Super looked up from her computer screen as if we'd interrupted something important.

'Are you here to tell me you know who has murdered three people by setting them on fire, including a former Met Officer?'

'It's Ged Wallace we'd like to talk to you about, ma'am.'

She stared right through me. 'Go on.'

'Do you remember him?'

Cane's lips turned up in a vague resemblance of a smile.

'I never forget my Officers, DI Flowers. What would you like to know?'

'What was he doing between June and September in 2010?' Jack said.

Her grin twisted into a laugh. 'That's very specific, DI Monroe.'

I explained to her about the missing records and what I thought they could signify.

'All three of our victims retired from work in late 2010; it's the only connection we have between them so far. They all mean something to our killer, so,' I glanced at Jack, 'we think Wallace might have been working on an investigation that links him to Green and Cole during that period.'

'A social worker, a crime reporter, and a copper – and you believe one of Wallace's cases connects them all.'

'It's a theory, ma'am,' Jack said.

'But we got nothing from Green's colleagues in social services,' I said, 'and there were no leads in Cole's newspaper clippings.'

'Which is why you're pinning all your hopes on Wallace's missing files and my memory?'

I nodded. 'Yes, ma'am.'

'Well, I've got good and bad news for you.' Her smile disappeared. 'I remember that period well and why I took Ged off the cases he was working on. There was a heightened terrorist alert across the country in the latter half of 2010, no more so than in London.'

She didn't expand upon that, but I understood what she meant.

'So Wallace was one of the officer's directed towards prevention of terrorism investigations?'

'He was,' Cane said. 'Ged had forty years of experience on criminal cases in the capital and knew how to work across varied and different communities. He was invaluable in the anti-terrorist work the Met completed that year.'

'If that's the good news, what's the bad?' Jack said.

'I can't remember what he was working on. If he didn't record it on the PNC or the PND, I can only assume he thought it wasn't worthwhile.'

She was correct; it was bad. And Wallace should have kept details of his investigations, regardless of whether he deemed them worthy. I had one last hope Cane might prove helpful.

'What about the officers who worked with Wallace?'

'There will be a record of that on the system somewhere if you look hard enough, Jennifer.'

With that, she turned back to her screen and dismissed us without saying so. Jack followed me out of her office.

'Does this mean we have to suffer looking through more computer files?'

'We should go over the evidence from the murder scenes again. Now we know a woman is involved.'

He shrugged and sighed as we stepped into the office.

We analysed the forensic details once more, gazing at the crime scene photos until my head hurt. I was about to put my fist through the monitor when Grealish returned with news. She placed scans of Wallace's credit cards on the desk.

'I began by working backwards by date to compare the accounts. When nothing significant showed up after I'd trawled through six months on each card, I knew it would take forever unless I tried a different tack.'

It was my turn to rub at the pain in the back of my neck.

'And what was that, Constable?'

Grealish struggled to control her grin.

'I used Wallace's dates of missing information from 2010 and checked on the twelve months after those.' Her teeth were sparkling a brilliant white. 'And I discovered something interesting.'

She paused for a response, which Jack provided.

'Well, don't keep us in suspenders, Constable.'

'Within those twelve months, each account had £25,000 worth of deposits.'

He whistled. 'A hundred grand from somewhere. Could you tell where the cash came from?'

Grealish nodded. 'I spoke to the managers at each of the banks, only one of whom was employed there at the time, but they all said the same thing: the money was transferred from a bank in the Cayman Islands.'

It was my turn to whistle. 'Was it the same bank?'

'No, it was different each time, though I suspect if we check hard enough, we'll find they're all connected. I'll keep digging into it.'

Jack narrowed his eyes and stared at me. 'I hate dealing with bent coppers, even dead ones.'

I knew how he felt. 'The important questions are: who paid him and why?'

He pushed the scans of the credit cards to the side. 'There has to be a connection to that investigation he had to quit.'

'I agree, partner, but where does our murderous fire-woman come into it?'

He rubbed at his neck again. 'I don't know, but I owe her one.'

The crime scene photos on the computer gave me a headache. The social worker died in her chair, turned to ash as the blaze ripped through her in seconds. The speed of death from being burned alive depended on the size of the fire. Those involved in a public burning would probably die from breathing carbon monoxide before the flames got them. A smaller fire could last a long time. If the fire didn't reach the head, death would occur because of the damage done and the body's response to it, but a person could also last hours before dying from blood loss or organ failure. If someone poured fuel over the victim, the death was usually within a minute because of them breathing in the fumes and smoke. The pain and trauma often caused the person to pass out quickly, and death soon followed.

Green's death must have been quick because it looked like she didn't move at all in that chair. But it was different for the private investigator, the former journalist. Not all of him went up in flames, as was clear from the photos. Parts of him didn't burn entirely or turn into a pile of ash like the social worker; both of his hands were only partially burnt as if he'd beaten them on the desk to put out the flames, which was how he could write those letters into the desk.

'Pain.'

Jack peered over the top of his computer screen. 'What did you say, partner?'

'I'm looking at the photos from the office of the private investigator again. Do you have them on your monitor?'

'I do. You're wondering why he wrote that word, aren't you?'

'It makes little sense. Why write that? He must have been in excruciating agony.' I'd spilt a small amount of soup on my hand last year and it was the worst pain I'd ever felt; well, apart from childbirth. The burning soup was on my flesh for less than a second, but it was so bad I had to leave that hand in cold water for eight hours. There was no scar, but I continued to feel the pain for days after.

'I'm guessing he wasn't thinking straight at that point.'

'I disagree, Jack.' I peered so hard at the image, at the letters, I felt them pressing against the front of my skull.

PAIN.

PAIN.

PAIN.

Or was it?

'You should have a rest, Jen. It might seem clearer in the morning.'

He was right, but I couldn't spend another sleepless night dwelling on this.

'Look at the photo, Jack. Maybe the letter I is part of the N.'

'What, so he wrote the word PAN?' His eyebrows narrowed in disagreement. 'As in the Greek god?'

I shook my head. 'No. Pan as in short for Pandora.'

He swung his chair around from the desk and pointed his pen at me.

'If that's true, it would help us a lot.'

'Because Pandora is a unique female name?'

He nodded. 'And if there's someone in the system with that name, it could be a proper lead.'

It took me five minutes to search the records for females called Pandora living in London with a criminal conviction in the last fifteen years. The Police National Computer kept all information until an individual's 100th birth date and surprised me with the results.

'There's more than one, Jack.'

His groan shook the monitor on his desk. 'Give me the bad news.'

'It's okay; the search came back with four names: Pandora Sutch, thirty-four, convicted for being drunk and disorderly; Pandora Gideon, twenty-eight, guilty of armed robbery; Pandora Lilly, forty-five, banged up for assault with a deadly weapon and GBH; and Pandora Lewis, forty-three,, convicted of murder.'

His eyes bulged. 'Was arson involved with Lewis?'

I scrolled through the details. 'No. She stabbed her estranged husband when he tried to strangle her.'

'Do we have photos of them?'

I shook my head. 'Not that I can see.'

Jack stood and put his jacket on. 'We better check all of them.'

'It will be quicker if we split up. So you take Constable Sutton to see Sutch and Gideon while Grealish and I speak to the other two.'

Sutton got the addresses from the database and we set off to find our Pandora.

33 PANDORA: THE TRUTH

I didn't go straight into my flat, striding across the road to rest at the bench of the three wise monkeys. Instead, I sat for a few minutes, feeling the notebook inside my now dry jacket. The bench had been a gift to the council from a local artist. My hand trembled as I placed my fingers on the head of the closest monkey, wondering which I'd rather be – the one that sees, speaks or hears no evil?

The sun warmed my face as I thought of those who saw and heard evil deeds, but never spoke of them. They deserved to be punished; that was unarguable. Many felt the same way as me, but were fearful of speaking up; I knew this from experience.

'Look at those fucking muppets.'

It wasn't so much his choice of words that shook me from my reverie, but the invective thick in every syllable. He'd crept up on me without a sound, walking over the grass to stand by my side as we stared across the road. I expected to see dancing television puppets, but there was a group of refugees new to the area.

'What?'

I'd heard what he'd said, but couldn't think of anything else to say. He was a big man who looked to be in his mid-twenties, possessed of one of those hipster beards and lopsided haircuts most young men favoured nowadays. He wore a t-shirt that exposed muscular arms covered with tattoos that resembled runic symbols. Both of my legs could have fitted inside one of his.

'Those foreign bastards there, taking our jobs and houses.'

I didn't dare to tell him they weren't allowed to work – their current status was of non-people – and had been given the smallest and dirtiest places to live. I knew all this because I'd once worked as a volunteer for the refugee service.

If my head had been in a better place, I might have attempted to educate him, but I never got the chance. Instead, he pulled out a blade from somewhere and waved it in my face.

'They're a disease that needs cutting out of our community.'

It was larger than a knife, but smaller than a sword. My mind slipped into the past, and I remembered seeing something similar in an old Hollywood movie, some black and white adventure nonsense where white men civilised dark continents. I saw my reflection staring at me as he pushed the weapon closer to my face. I appeared pale and tired, shadowy bags living under my soft blue eyes like garbage dumped in an alley.

My journey would be over soon, so I could leave him to whatever he was about to do, couldn't I?

Seeing evil and letting it thrive.

I stood and touched his arm. 'You should go home, son. You must have loved ones waiting for you.'

His eyes were burning red and I recognised the chemical influence behind them.

'I have a wife and daughter,' he said.

A daughter.

I moved my hand closer to the blade. 'You should be with them. If you do something terrible now, you'll leave them all alone to deal with the struggles of this life. Trust me; you don't want that to happen.'

My fingers were on the weapon, trembling as I expected him to push me aside.

But he must have seen the truth in my eyes because he dropped the blade and turned from me. I watched him walk away before picking it up, dropping it through the gutter and into the sewer.

I breathed a sigh of relief as I headed into my flat.

Was it only a temporary postponement of tragedy I'd made for him and those he'd wanted to hurt?

I removed my jacket and took out Wallace's notebook, placing it on the table next to my Murder Diary, knowing that everything in this life was temporary.

My guts told me to eat before I did anything else. Understanding this wasn't another delaying tactic on my part, I went to the kitchen and made toast, glancing out of the window to ensure the troubled young man hadn't returned, but all was quiet outside.

Hot butter crumbled in my mouth as I steadied my twitching nerves. The copper's book would provide me with the truth one way or the other. I finished the toast and went to the living room, sitting at the table before running my hand over Wallace's secret records.

Then I picked it up and opened it to the first page.

It was all there, everything I knew to be true, but hidden by Green, Cole, Wallace and others. And it was the truth about the others that made my legs shake, and the blood boil in my veins.

I threw the book across the room, knocking ornaments off the shelves and to the floor. My feet crushed them even further as I raged against the world, shouting at my invisible enemies and destroying everything close to me. Then I fell to my knees, finally understanding that it was I who'd done all this, who'd destroyed everything close to me.

I grabbed Wallace's notebook, pulling it to my chest before peering at the page, still unbelieving at the name I'd found in his words.

My body shivered as I got up, turning to retrieve my jacket. I put the notebook into my pocket and glanced at what I'd done. That's when I saw the broken frame amongst the debris. I bent down and removed the photo from it, staring at my loss even though her image was always in my head.

Now was the last leg of my journey.

My final truth would come to those who'd hidden theirs for so long.

34 JEN: THE PAST

Jack and Sutton headed for Camberwell while I drove to Paddington. The smell of petrol lingered at the back of my head as Constable Grealish checked her phone, still searching for those connections in the Cayman Islands. We were ten minutes away when Grealish said she had an update.

'Somebody just tagged Pandora Lilly in a photo uploaded to Facebook.'

I stopped at a red light and she showed me the image on her mobile. The caption described it as an anniversary celebration at work for Pandora. There was more than one photo and the individuals weren't identified in them, but when I took the phone and flicked through them, that smell of fiery death nearly overpowered me. The traffic lights turned green, but I couldn't move, fixed on Pandora: even with half of her face covered by that scarf, I'd recognise those eyes anywhere.

Car horns blared around me as I changed the GPS directions and returned Grealish's phone to her.

'Text Jack that link and tell him to meet us at Pandora Lilly's place.'

She did that as I sped through London, my mind fixed only on one thing and ignoring the imaginary smell of petrol.

We reached the flats first.

'Should we call for Armed Response, ma'am?'

I shook my head. 'Let's confirm she's here. We don't want them coming out for nothing.'

The road swung round into a large car park. I ignored the warning signs promising fines for cars without valid permits and led Grealish to the entrance. You needed a code to get in if you weren't buzzing the resident, and Grealish had got it from the landlords before we'd left. She punched it in and we entered, greeted by an aroma of cleaning fluids and damp. We headed for the lifts. There were two sets, one for the even floors, one for the odd. And both were out of order. Which meant we were walking up ten flights. Grealish undid the buttons on her jacket.

'Good job I go to the gym five times a week.'

And here was me with an inch of fat fighting its way out of the top of my trousers. Too many takeaways and lack of exercise had led to this, me clutching my chest by the time we were halfway there. Two teenage girls bundled past us down the steps, giggling through enough makeup to sink a battleship at my struggles, my heart throbbing as if it was about to burst.

When we reached the tenth floor, it was as if I'd gone twelve rounds in the boxing ring. I couldn't see my face, but it was hot to touch. Grealish must have noticed my difficulty.

'Are you okay, ma'am?'

The sweat from my forehead came away like a river in

my hand. This was more than being unfit. Perhaps I'd caught a bug somewhere.

'I'm fine. Have you heard from DI Monroe?'

She nodded. 'Constable Sutton said they'd be here soon.'

'Warn them about the lifts.'

I moved to flat 105, with no plan of getting inside without knocking on the door. However, before I could do that, someone stepped out of the neighbouring flat.

'She's not in.'

The voice stuttered through cracked lips, belonging to a woman closer to death than life. She possessed Rapunzel's hair, grey as an elephant with the skin to match. I showed her my ID.

'Do you mean Pandora?'

Her fingers trembled as she raised a hand to me. 'Pandora was shouting at someone, louder than her normal racket, and then I heard the furniture crashing against the wall and the sound of breaking glass. Then she sprinted from the flat as if it was on fire.'

I placed my palm on the door, fearing heat but getting nothing but the chill of the wood. Then, as I pressed harder, it swung open. There was no aroma of fire or burning, no smell of death as I spoke to Grealish.

'Take the neighbour inside and get a statement. I'll wait for the others to arrive.'

She narrowed her eyes at me. 'Are you sure, ma'am?'

'I am. Now go ahead.'

Grealish took the woman inside. As soon as the door closed, I stepped into Pandora's flat, seeing destruction everywhere. Broken ornaments littered the entrance, bits of small Victorian men and women lying over the carpet. I dodged their cracked eyes and moved into the living room.

A smashed chair lay next to what remained of a coffee table, with splintered wood scattered up to the floorboards under the window. Someone had thrust a poker through the TV screen while books and magazines were torn and open across the room.

There were no signs of blood, no evidence more than one person had caused the damage. I checked the bathroom and bedroom, both clean, which meant Pandora must have done this herself, in a rage at something.

But at what?

I removed a pen from my pocket and knelt forward, peering at the debris covering the carpet. I poked at it between the destruction until I'd moved enough out of the way to see the splintered but empty photo frame. Then, closer to the ground, I got a hit of a familiar aroma: petrol.

My reflexes kicked in, legs springing up with a jolt. It was only a faint smell, somewhere under the pile on the floor, and not enough to set a blaze alight in seconds. At least I hoped so. The sweat had vanished from me and I could breathe without wanting to throw up. Whatever had made me react like that was gone. Even so, the stink of petrol had jolted me.

I gazed at the empty photo frame. Then the image of Pandora at her work party flashed across the back of my eyes, focusing on the enigmatic smile she'd given the camera. I could barely process it before it changed to the memory of me in that petrol-soaked basement and the flickering match in her hand.

Wallace's police notebook, the one she'd waved at me – had she found something in it which triggered this outburst of destruction? What was it in her past she was fighting against?

I returned to the bedroom and got my answer. At the

bottom of the wardrobe was an album full of family photos underneath a pile of clothes. I slipped my protective gloves over my hands and went through it: Pandora with a newborn baby, then her with a small child, and the kid as a teenager with Pandora. The girl looked about fifteen in the photos, about Abbey's age, but there were no others of her older than that.

The rest of the album contained newspaper cuttings about missing kids in London, including a piece written by James Cole, one we hadn't found amongst those many boxes of his journalism. I read the details, making a mental note of the six teenagers, boys and girls, who'd disappeared. And the last name on the list was Catherine: Pandora's daughter.

I removed the album and sat on the bed, the kids' names glued to my brain. The article's date was two months after Pandora's arrest for assault with a deadly weapon and GBH against the father of her child. I used my phone to take photos of every page. By the time I'd finished, Jack was behind me.

'You should have waited for backup, Jen.'

'Did you see the damage in the living room?'

Of course he had. What a stupid thing to say.

'Was there a fight here?'

I repeated what the neighbour had told us. 'Where are Sutton and Grealish?'

'They've gone to the station. Grealish thinks she has a lead on the Cayman banks and wants to check the financial accounts of the social worker and journalist.'

I heard the words, but didn't process them, too busy staring at the photos of mother and daughter, with so many of them similar to ones of Abbey and me taken over the years: smiling at the park; laughing together; running on the beach; and trawling through Camden Market. Perhaps they'd walked near us there in the past.

Forensics arrived fifteen minutes later, and Jack drove us back to the station. Sutton and Grealish were busy with their computers, and I left them to it. Jack put an alert out for Pandora while I went over her records again, reading through what history we had on her, from birth and school-days up to the point of her imprisonment.

The first thing I read was about the death of her parents in a car accident. Then there were reports of juvenile infractions, problems with foster families, and care homes as she was shuffled across the city. She'd attended at least a dozen secondary schools in that time, and as I scanned down the list, I tried to imagine how disruptive it must have all been for her, as well as the emotional upheaval.

All of which would have contributed to her homeless-ness. After that, there was nothing until 2010 and her imprisonment. She'd attacked the father of her child after making allegations of domestic abuse against him.

And that was the year her daughter had disappeared. Catherine was fifteen and living with her dad when it happened. No one had seen her since, and the police had stopped looking a long time ago. They'd questioned the father, but nothing had come from it.

I tried to put myself in her place, picturing what I'd do to find Abbey if she was missing, thinking what it must have been like to be stuck behind bars and unable to do anything for your child.

After ten years, it was doubtful Pandora's daughter was still alive. Perhaps with her early life and time in prison, she'd always lived on the edge, but discovering something terrible might have happened to Catherine must have tipped her over it.

And tipped her into murder.

Would I act the same in that situation? Would I kill for my daughter? I wanted to think I wouldn't, that no matter how distraught I was, I couldn't sink to that. But experience had taught me that violence is in all of us, simmering below the veneer of respectability and civilised living. So, deep down, I didn't know how I'd react if something terrible happened to Abbey.

And if I knew others were responsible for that terrible act, that they were culpable by involvement or silence, what would I do then?

I'd seek justice, but not death. Punishment yes, vengeance no.

All these thoughts were flowing through my head like a turbulent river intent on drowning me when Constable Grealish jumped out of her chair. The cobwebs melted from my brain as she approached.

'I've found the connection.'

We all stared at her, but only Jack spoke.

'You nearly gave me a heart attack, Constable.'

'Sorry, sir.' She went to the printer to retrieve a document. 'Wallace's Cayman connections are too entwined to untangle them, but the other two victims weren't so conscientious about their financial accounts.'

There were four copies of what Grealish had found, and she handed us one each. I saw a load of numbers and names I didn't recognise.

'You'll have to decipher this for me, Jackie.'

She pointed at the last paragraph. 'Watkins Financial Services made payments to both Green and Cole over five years, totalling £100,000 for each of them.'

I peered at the name until my head hurt.

'Am I supposed to know Watkins Financial Services?'

'Probably not, but you'll recognise the company that owns them: Randolph Industries.'

Jack nearly fell out of his chair. 'Robert Randolph, the tech multi-millionaire?'

'The same, sir.' She looked at me. 'What shall we do about him?'

'Go to his mansion and bring him here.'

Jack stared at me. 'And how do we get him to accompany us?'

'Tell him we have evidence linking one of his companies to three murders. If that doesn't convince him, then drop a hint that the news might be leaked to the media. I'm sure he wouldn't want his reputation ruined.'

I watched them leave, then I returned to Pandora's life on the computer, though it was him I was thinking about.

Robert Randolph. The man I'd seen at Abbey's football match.

35 JEN: THE MONEY

An hour later, Randolph was sitting next to his lawyer in an interview room while Jack and I stood in the corridor. I peered at the multi-millionaire businessman through the window, impressed by his suave coolness. If someone had cloned George Clooney and given him a posh English accent, that would be Randolph. The sheen of his grey hair complemented the sparkling blue of his eyes. He appeared unruffled as if waiting for his tailor to arrive.

I spoke to Jack. 'Did he give you any trouble?'

He shook his head. 'Not even a whimper. It was the lawyer spitting fire and brimstone and threatening lawsuits. He soon calmed down when I mentioned we hadn't spoken to the media yet.'

'It's only a matter of time before someone discovers he's here, and then holy hell will break out.'

I watched Randolph through the glass, trying to fathom out what was going on behind that calm expression. He gazed at his fingers as if he was without a care in the world.

It was time to give him something to worry about.

Jack went in first and made the introductions,

explaining Randolph was only there to help with our enquiries. For now. I sat down and glanced at the red lights above us, indicating the cameras were recording. Then I removed two photos from the folder in my hand and pushed one towards him.

'Do you recognise this woman, Mr Randolph?'

He barely registered the image, more concerned with a tiny spot of dirt underneath his fingernails. Perhaps it was ash. Then he spent a minute scrutinising the photo.

'I meet many people, Inspector, but I don't know her.'

I expected him to ask who she was, but he didn't – instead removing the offending dirt and dropping it to the floor. I showed him the second image from the album I'd found in Pandora's flat. He gazed at mother and daughter smiling into the camera, but he didn't blink.

'What about here, with this girl? Do you know either of them?'

He turned to face me properly for the first time since I'd sat down. His smile was broader than the horizon and as warm as the sun. At least initially. After thirty seconds of silence, I noticed a slight waver in his top lip and watched as he wiped the moisture from his mouth.

'I can't say I do, Inspector.'

The lawyer piped up. 'What's this all about? I'm one step from informing the media about this flagrant disregard of my client's civil liberties.'

Jack smirked and removed his phone. 'Here, you can use this.'

Randolph patted his lawyer on the arm. 'Now, now, Jacob. Let's allow the Inspectors to enlighten us in their own time. I'm sure this must be important for them to ask me to come here.'

The gleam in his eyes told me I'd got it wrong about

him. It wasn't that he didn't care about this intrusion into his life; he was enjoying it.

'The names Pandora and Catherine Lilly mean nothing to you, Mr Randolph?'

He picked up the photo of mother and daughter, brought it closer to his face, and then shook his head.

'I'm afraid not, Inspector Flowers.' He returned it to the table. 'Has something happened to them?'

I ignored his question and removed another document from the folder. It was the financial details of the three victims, and I placed it in front of him.

'Do these mean anything to you, Mr Randolph?'

His shrug dislodged a stray grey hair from his forehead. He left it there as he spoke, hanging near his eyes like an upside-down exclamation point.

'I've never been very good with numbers. Perhaps you should show them to my accountant.'

Jack leant towards him. 'Do you know of Watkins Financial Services?'

Randolph stared at Jack as if he was stuck to the bottom of his shoe.

'Do they help you with your taxes, Inspector?'

I pointed to the paper. 'Watkins Financial Services paid £100,000 over two years into each of these accounts: Betty Green and James Cole. Do you know these people?'

Jack placed their photos on the table.

Randolph moved closer and bent his head towards the images. Then he gave the same answer.

'I don't know them or anything about their financial accounts.'

Jack's eye twitched as he spoke. 'Do you know Ged Wallace?'

'I've never heard of him.'

I glanced at the red light flickering above us.

'Do you have any dealings with banks in the Cayman Islands?'

He puffed out his cheeks in a show he was finally getting irritated.

'I told you I have nothing to do with the financial side of my business.'

I pointed at the paper. 'And you know nothing about Watkins Financial Services?'

'Haven't I already said that?' His voice sounded as if he was speaking through broken glass.

'Randolph Industries owns Watkins Financial Services. That is your company, isn't it, Mr Randolph?'

His laugh was unnerving, like a large bellows thrust into your face.

'Is that what this is all about?' He removed a handkerchief from his top pocket and wiped at his eyes. 'Randolph Industries is a vast umbrella business, Inspector Flowers. There are hundreds of companies and organisations beneath it. I don't know of or involve myself with most of them.'

Jack didn't sound convinced. 'Even when they're dishing out a hundred grand to people like sweets in a candy shop?'

'I told you. Somebody else handles all of that.'

'Yes,' I said. 'It's your accountant.'

'No, he wouldn't deal with most of those businesses. So I leave that to someone I trust completely.'

I leant closer to him. 'And who is that?'

He laughed again. 'Why, my wife, of course.'

'Your wife?' Jack said.

Randolph appeared to relax into his chair.

'Yes. Grace deals with ninety per cent of the business.

I've never had a head for finances or organising things, but she's brilliant at it.' He placed both hands on the desk. 'Grace has saved me millions over the years.' Then he glanced at the lawyer. 'All legal, of course.'

He was enjoying himself again and it annoyed me. Then I pictured him and his wife at Abbey's match.

'Is this so you can spend more time on your hobbies, like watching a girls' football team?'

He grimaced. 'Oh no, I have no interest in sports. That's Grace's domain. She's always been one for promoting activities for women and girls, especially in those fields seen as male bastions. She gives her favourite girls' team a lot of time and money.'

'What's the name of the football team your wife funds through Randolph Industries?'

He narrowed his eyes at me. 'That's Goodwood Girls.'

Something cold clutched at my heart. 'Why them?'

He looked at me as if I was an idiot, and maybe I was.

'Because that's where she went to school, Goodwood Academy. It wasn't an Academy then, of course, just your average state school. I think she had a hard time there because it was quite sexist, even with the staff, so she was determined to help the girls there now.'

The chill continued to ripple through me as my mind returned to the list of schools Pandora Lilly had attended during her turbulent childhood.

'How old is your wife, Mr Randolph?'

His grin irritated me. 'Grace? Well, you won't believe it because she looks a good ten years younger than she is, but she'll be forty-five this year.'

I had to stop myself from jumping out of the chair and running from the room. I got the photo and showed it to him again.

'Are you sure you don't know this woman, Mr Randolph?'

His eyes glazed over as he shook his head.

'I keep telling you no. Who is she anyway?'

I left the photo there. 'That's Pandora Lilly. She's murdered three people by burning them alive, and I think your wife is next on her kill list.'

The colour drained from his face. 'Grace? Why would she want to murder Grace?'

'I believe she thinks Grace is connected to the disappearance of her daughter Catherine in 2010. Pandora and Grace were in the same year at school.'

'That's ridiculous. Why would she be involved in such a thing?'

'I don't know, but we need to find out. Where is your wife now?'

His eyes were bulging, that previously calm demeanour having vanished.

'She'll be at her beauty parlour. It's one business she runs, and Grace goes there three or four times a week for her treatments.'

He provided the address and we left him to give a statement to Constable Grealish. Jack followed me to my desk, where I gazed at Pandora's details on my computer.

'You believe his wife is behind those missing kids in 2010?'

'It doesn't matter what we think, but Pandora believes it.' I pointed at the screen. 'Look at this.'

He stepped over and stared at what I was looking at.

'They both went to the same school, this Goodwood Academy, which used to be called Goodwood Secondary. It doesn't mean she's involved in this.' He pushed his face closer to the computer, and then pulled back. 'Does it?'

'It's not a coincidence, Jack. I believed Randolph when he said he knew nothing about his businesses and the payments to the victims. Someone else must have made them, and that, according to him, was his wife. And now we know Grace was at the same school with Pandora.'

'How many kids go to Abbey's school, Jen?'

'About a thousand, with two hundred in her year group.'

'And she'll only know a small amount of those kids, won't she?'

'Yes, I get it, Jack, but this is more than a fluke. I think Pandora discovered something in Wallace's police notebook which angered her enough to damage her flat. So what if she found out, like Wallace, Green, and Cole did, that Grace Randolph was involved in her daughter's disappearance? Perhaps they were friends at school. Maybe she thought Grace would look after Catherine while she was in prison.'

'We're just guessing here, Jen.'

'Of course we are, which is why we need to speak to Grace Randolph.' I nodded at Constable Sutton. 'Do we have the address of that beauty parlour?'

'I've sent it to your phone, ma'am.'

She had. Now we had to go to one of the posher parts of London.

36 PANDORA: THE REUNION

A s I stumbled through the city, a thousand tiny Victorian soldiers were stabbing the back of my eyes with their bayonets as a cacophony of elephants cried inside my ears. My nostrils were clogged with the aroma of dead fish, the insides of my mouth transformed into the seventh level of Hell.

I glanced at my reflection in the shop windows as I staggered through the streets, seeing a haggard-looking woman staring back at me. The public kept out of my way, but I wasn't aware of them, only of my own failings.

But I didn't just blame myself.

There was an illness in the city – in the world – not one of chemistry or biology unless you believed evil was inherent inside human DNA. And perhaps it was. To make it worse, it was accompanied by a secondary disease, that of silence. These twin ailments didn't affect everyone, but they affected enough. All my life, I'd tried to view these people as no better than the living dead, walking emotional corpses to be avoided. They shuffled around and glared at anyone not like them, so I'd made myself invisible to their gaze.

Or so I'd thought.

Instead, I'd only deluded myself about what had been in front of my eyes all the time.

Perhaps it would have been different if my parents hadn't died in that car crash, but I had my doubts after what so many had told me in prison about the nature of evil.

Evil isn't a thing. It is neither born nor created. It is what we label something we find unacceptable. Numerous people would say my actions were evil, to kill as I had, and I'd agree with them, but those I'd killed had also committed evil acts by doing nothing when they knew others were suffering.

It was the same when I ended up behind bars. Prison was my fault, I didn't deny that, but I'd had no choice. I'd gone to the police and social services several times about him, but was always worried they'd remove Catherine from me and leave him alone with her. And in the end, the authorities did nothing, not even warning him about his violent behaviour.

So I had to take matters into my own hands.

I'd loved him at first and thought he'd loved me, but that attraction soon wore off once Catherine arrived, and he believed I loved her more than him. He wasn't wrong, of course.

When we'd met, his hair had been short and brown, curling up at the edges as if desperate to get away from his head. It had reminded me of a dog my parents had bought me. I should have known then what was to come as they had similar personalities: quick to temper with a permanent sense of grievance. At first, I'd been mesmerised by his eyes, but eventually, they came to resemble the Devil's gaze, something like witchcraft. They followed me around the room. And down the corridor. And into the cupboard that I hid in. And into my dreams, that became nightmares.

I never think of Catherine's father's name now, but he was a talentless musician. He couldn't sing, but he knew how to rewrite history. He denied his violence against me and kept on denying it as I raised the hammer above my head.

The weight of it in my hand had comforted me, as did seeing his blood turn the room crimson. The red was still behind my eyes as I twisted away from my reflection, stumbling down a kerb. Expletives fell from my lips as I dropped to the ground, hitting the concrete hard.

Tommy's face peered down at me as I lay there. Was this the exact spot where I'd saved his life?

And I'd never gone back to visit him in the hospital.

Somebody else I'd let down.

The cars beeped their horns and avoided my head. I wanted to stay there and never get up until I heard her voice calling to me from above.

You need help, Mum. You should do it for me.

But everything I'd done was for her, for Catherine.

And it wasn't her speaking, but a woman holding out her hand to lift me. So I took it.

'Are you okay?' she said.

I nodded my thanks and continued marching towards the reunion with my past – a meeting with those I'd trusted to look after my daughter.

Catherine had always been with me, even after she'd disappeared, but I'd known her voice in my head was only my guilt trying to comfort me. And that meant the whisper I heard in my ear wasn't her telling me to turn back, to seek help, but another part of my brain that knew where my journey would end.

Where it would finish for all of us.

Lulu's Beauty Emporium was in Spitalfields, and I browsed its website as Jack drove us there. We parked on the double yellow lines outside the front and got out of the car. I instructed Sutton and Grealish to go to the back of the premises.

'You think Grace Randolph will do a runner?' he said.

'No. But if Pandora is already here, we need to cover all the exits. If Randolph is the last piece in her murder jigsaw and she gets away, we might never see her again.'

When we entered, the place was heaving, full of customers getting bits of them improved. Most were women of all ages, but I spotted a few men. Jack stared at one of them and rubbed his forehead.

'That reminds me, I need to get my eyebrows waxed.'

For as long as I'd known him, he'd always been fastidious in his grooming, but since he'd started dating a woman half his age, he'd become even more fixated on his appearance.

'If we save Grace Randolph from a fiery death, she might give you a discount.'

My frivolous reply was to cover the nagging pain in the back of my head. There was something I was missing here and it bothered me. One of the staff approached us, a woman in her early twenties who looked like she'd had one too many injections into her cheeks. Behind her was a giant Buddha statue, along with stacks of creams and other beauty products. The smell of wax lingered in the air, and it felt like I was standing in the door of a microwave set to maximum heat.

'Do you have an appointment?' I shook my head, and she continued speaking before I could reply. 'Then I'm sorry, but we're full for the day. You'll need to ring later and book a session.' She peered at Jack, and then returned to me. 'Is it a little facial waxing you require?'

I showed her my ID.

'Is Grace Randolph here?'

She clutched at her chest, her pink hair wobbling as her head moved.

'Oh, the boss, yes, she's in the backroom with her accountant.'

'Her accountant?'

'Yeah, not the usual one. It's some woman I haven't seen before.'

Jack showed her a photo of Pandora. 'Is this her?'

She nodded. 'Though she looks different now, with large bags under her eyes.'

One of her colleagues glared at her.

'Can you show us where they are?' I said.

'Of course.'

She turned around and we followed, with Jack whispering at my side.

'What if she's already spread the petrol? Shouldn't we empty this place?'

He was right. I placed my hand on our guide's shoulder and stopped walking. She gazed at me, eyes bulging like a frog's. Perhaps she thought I was going to arrest her.

'You need to get everybody out and close this place.'

We didn't know if Pandora was there, but we couldn't take the risk.

'Is... is something wrong?'

'We don't know, but it's better to be safe than sorry, don't you think?'

She appeared to consider the situation, and I wondered what terrible events were running through her mind: a bomb or terrorist, perhaps a gang of people traffickers, but not your everyday arsonist serial killer.

'What will Mrs Randolph say?'

Jack added his calming voice. 'It's her orders we're acting on.'

Her mouth formed a perfect O. Then the sound appeared.

'Oh. We better leave then.' She pointed to the end of the room. 'The boss is in the first room down the corridor.'

I moved first and Jack followed, ensuring the staff emptied the building. I received a text as we went from Sutton telling me they'd secured the exit. I told her to stay there unless she heard from me. The room was ahead of us, the windows frosted so you couldn't see inside. Jack stood next to me.

'Do we just walk in?'

I put my fingers on the handle. 'What choice do we have?'

The metal chilled my flesh as I pushed the door open. The room was bigger than it had appeared from the outside, stretching out to reach the building's end.

And it was empty.

Jack stepped in front of me. 'It looks like we missed her.'

I paused inside the entrance, scanning for any signs of life. Or death. A row of unfamiliar machines was lined up against the far wall with stacks of dangerous-looking chairs opposite.

'I'm not sure. What's that smell?'

He moved ahead of me, checking everywhere for Grace or Pandora.

'There are all kinds of chemicals in here, Jen. It could be any combination of them.'

'You don't think it smells like petrol?'

He shrugged. 'I suppose it could be, but it's not very strong, not like the other crime scenes.'

I listened to him while staring at the shadows at the rear, beyond the jungle of furniture and abandoned machinery. Then the darkness moved and Grace Randolph stepped out.

'How can I help you?'

Jack made to move forward, but I held him back, watching the tic in her eyelid and the way her fingers shook. She raised them to her face to touch her cheek.

'I'm Detective Inspector Flowers, Mrs Randolph, and this is my partner, Detective Inspector Monroe. Can we have a word with you?'

She glanced from me, staring at the machines at her side.

'I'm sorry, Inspectors, I'm swamped at the moment. The business has really taken off the last month, and I have no spare time at all.' She appeared to relax. 'My husband isn't happy about me being away from home so much, but he forgets I'm making money for both of us.' She ran a finger over the hairdryer next to her and I could smell the dust from where I stood. 'I can come down to the station later if that's okay?'

'This is urgent, Mrs Randolph. We need to speak to you now.'

She touched her cheek as if there was something hidden beneath her skin.

'Well, okay, but you should stay where you are. I've spent too much time outside watching girls' football matches and I think I've caught a nasty cold.' She glanced at Jack. 'I wouldn't want to give it to you or your partner. Heaven knows what the police would do to me then.' Her laugh was nervous, with her eyes blinking at a rapid pace.

I resisted the urge to move forward.

'Do you know a Pandora Lilly, Mrs Randolph?'

She twisted her mouth into an awkward shape. 'I don't think so.'

'You went to school with her at Goodwood Secondary, what is now the Goodwood Academy.'

'Oh my, I left there more than twenty-five years ago. I haven't seen any of my old chums since. I move in different circles now, you see.'

'What about Pandora's daughter, Catherine? Do you know her?'

She narrowed her eyes. 'I can't say I do, Inspector. Is she part of the Goodwood Girls football team I sponsor?'

'Catherine disappeared in 2010. She and several other teenagers went missing from the city. Are you sure you've never met her?'

Randolph inched closer to the shadows behind her.

'That's such a long time ago, Inspector. I mean, I can barely remember what I did last week.' She giggled, appearing more like a schoolgirl than a grown woman.

'Pandora thinks, somebody covered up her daughter's

disappearance, Grace, so she's seeking revenge, killing people by burning them alive. We believe you're next on her list. You're not safe here and you should come with us. Do you understand that?'

She went to move towards me until a hand pulled her back. It was quick and covered in darkness, but there was no mistaking what I saw.

'No, no, I'll be okay here.'

I glanced at Jack, watching him send a text I assumed was to the officers outside, telling them to call for reinforcements and the fire service. I peered into the dark gap behind Randolph.

'You might as well come out now, Pandora. You can't escape from this.'

The tension lingered in the air, the silence hanging heavily enough to sink the *Titanic*. It seemed to last for an eternity, but I watched the clock on the wall ticking off sixty seconds. Then she pushed Grace forward and came into the light, a spray container in one hand and a lighter in the other. There was no need for matches now.

G race recognised me as soon as I stepped into the beauty parlour. Of course, I knew of her marriage to Randolph and the riches it brought, but standing there reminded me of how we'd gone in different directions since school. It was strange, considering how good I'd been academically even though I'd moved around so many schools and homes. In contrast, Grace had always been one of those kids who couldn't be bothered to study or learn anything useful.

She spent ten minutes giving me the business tour, showing me people being plucked and waxed as if they were turkeys preparing for Christmas. The smell of chemicals gave me a headache, so I asked if we could go somewhere private.

'Of course, Pan.' She tapped on her nose. 'I've got a few goodies in the back. We can partake in them while we reminisce about the good old days.'

I smiled as she led me into a huge storage room, watching her and wondering if she knew why I was there. Perhaps this was all an act and she'd attack me once we were away from the others.

As I closed the door behind me, Grace went straight to a cupboard, removing a box of pills and a bottle of whisky. She poured out two large measures before popping a pill into her mouth.

I took the drink from her. 'Do you have a headache?'

She giggled as if we were back at that school.

'Don't you think, Pan, at our age, we need all the help we can get to stay young inside and outside?'

Grace offered me a pill, but I refused.

'I've seen what drugs do to people. I spent a decade in prison and witnessed how they ruined so many lives.'

She seemed shocked at what I'd said.

'You were in prison?'

'I attacked the man who'd been abusing me, hitting him with a hammer over fifty times.'

'Christ!' She put a hand to her face. 'Was he the one you met when we were teenagers, the older bloke? What was his name?'

'I've forgotten it, Grace. I don't need to think of him anymore.' The whisky warmed my throat as I readied myself for how much warmer it was going to get. 'He was a terrible person, but he gave me the only good thing I've ever had in my life.'

She giggled again. 'Did he buy you a house?'

I put the drink down and removed the photo from my pocket.

'This is Catherine, my daughter.'

My old friend stumbled forward to peer at the image.

'Oh, isn't she lovely? She looks just like you did as a teenager.'

'You don't remember her,' I said.

She was unsteady on her feet as she gazed at Catherine.

'You know, Pan, with the charity I'm involved in, with

the football, I've seen so many teenage girls over the years, their faces all blur into one.'

I narrowed my eyes at her denial of knowing Catherine and of my imprisonment.

She had to be lying.

'You were at my trial, Grace. You spoke in my defence.'

Her eyes bulged as she appeared to recall our shared past.

'Oh my God, yes. You nearly killed that bastard. You should have killed him. How the hell he got custody of poor Catherine, I'll never know.'

I pressed my fingers against my jacket, touching the gift I'd brought for her.

'So you remember my daughter?'

Grace put a hand on her chest. 'Catherine, yes; little Cat, as I used to call her.'

'Did you see her after my imprisonment?'

She shook her head, her eyes betraying she wasn't dizzy anymore.

'Oh no, I couldn't go anywhere near her father. He was such a brute.' She moved forward and touched my arm. 'I'm sorry, Pan, but you know how much of a scaredy-cat I am. Is Catherine okay? She must have children of her own now.'

I inched away from her. 'Catherine disappeared not long after my sentence. That's why I'm here.'

'Disappeared? That's terrible. It's always happening in London.'

Was it all still an act of hers, this denial?

'When I was in prison, Grace, I heard rumours about kids disappearing and a cover-up by influential people.'

She nodded at me. 'Yes, I've heard about such things – politicians and royalty getting away with terrible crimes. I think there's a lot of it going on, Pan, but what's it got to do with me?'

'One of my fellow inmates gave me a name of a social worker involved in the cover-up. So when I got out, I visited her. She pointed me towards a former journalist, and he led me to a retired bent copper. He didn't tell me much before I killed him, but I found his police notebook full of notes from the investigation he'd abandoned when somebody paid him off. And guess what I discovered in that notebook, Grace?'

Her face was frozen as if injected with a shed load of her beauty chemicals.

'What?'

I removed the petrol from my jacket.

'You, Grace. I found you.'

39 JEN: THE END

'I should have dealt with you in that bent copper's basement, but I can't kill the innocent.' She gazed right through me. 'Are you innocent, Detective Inspector?'

Could we rush her before she sprayed the petrol and ignited the lighter? I glanced at Jack and knew the same thoughts must have been running through his head. Then I answered her question.

'Most of the time, Pandora. Why don't you put the lighter down and tell us what this is all about?'

Her response was to push Randolph. Grace fell to her knees, crying out as her hands hit the ground. Before I could move, Pandora sprayed Randolph's back, arms, and legs with petrol. Then she covered the surrounding floor with the liquid. Finally, she flicked the lighter on as Jack and I moved forward.

'Don't come any further,' Pandora said.

'You'll go up in flames as well,' Jack said.

She laughed. 'I'm counting on it.' Then she sprayed the machines and boxes around them. If there were chemicals in the containers, the whole place would go up. 'I'm not going back to prison.'

I moved an inch closer to my possible death.

'You know this is wrong, Pandora. What would your daughter think?'

Her fiery red eyes fixed on me as she put her foot on Randolph's spine and pushed her to the floor.

'Why don't we let Grace tell you about Catherine?'

Randolph spluttered and coughed, one hand reaching for her throat as she craned her neck to look at me.

'It was all an accident.'

I knelt to get eye contact with her, noticing Jack using his phone to record everything.

'Tell me how this started, Grace.'

Her eyes glazed over as she spoke.

'Once I married Robert and he let me do what I wanted with the money, I had to give something back to the community.' She stared beyond me, glancing around the room. 'It wasn't in here, but a building we had over the river. I tried to help a runaway, but she got the wrong idea when she saw him.' She stopped to look at her hand. 'And then the girl fell and hit her head on the side of the desk. The blood... the blood was everywhere.'

I peered straight into her eyes.

'That sounds like an accident, Grace. Why didn't you report it to the police?'

She continued to stare into her palm. 'It was the blood. It cleansed me.' She twisted towards me. 'I tried to pick the girl up, but got her blood all over me. It covered my hands for so long, it dried on my skin, and when I washed it away, do you know what I discovered?'

I didn't like where this was heading. 'What did you find, Grace?'

Her fear had gone, replaced with a sparkle in her eyes.

'My flesh was beautiful, revitalised by that girl's blood.' She pushed herself up and I stood as well. Pandora was motionless behind her. 'So I researched the healing properties of blood and knew what to do.'

Her eyes were manic now; her mind possessed of thoughts no sane person could understand.

'What did you do, Grace?'

She held up her hands and petrol dripped from her arms.

'I had no choice then, not if I wanted to stay beautiful forever.' She placed two fingers on her face. 'It's so much better than Botox.'

Pandora put her hand on the back of Randolph's neck.

'What happened to Catherine?'

Randolph squirmed from her grasp, apparently uncaring about her fate.

'I didn't even know who she was, Pan. He brought them to me, like all the others.' Her eyes narrowed. 'I didn't know what he did with them first, terrible things probably, but it was too late by then. I couldn't go back.' She looked at her hands again. 'And anyway, they were only runaways; they wouldn't have been happy.'

Pandora punched Randolph in the back of her head and knocked her to the floor, her face burning red.

'I was in prison then. I couldn't look after Catherine.'

Her hand trembled, her fingers twitching and the lighter ready to fall.

I stepped forward. 'Did Robert help you with this, Grace?'

She rolled on her back and laughed.

'No, no, Bob wouldn't hurt a fly. It was Declan, my bodyguard.' She gripped her chest. 'Bob recruited him from some criminal gang, but he was good at his job. And he's a loyal servant to me.'

I gazed into her eyes and saw nothing normal there.

Pandora lowered her shaking hand. 'So you admit to it all, killing my daughter and others?'

Randolph stopped moving, peering into the rafters as she spoke. 'Everything I said is true.'

Pandora knelt next to her. 'Then you deserve this justice.'

I moved close enough to feel the flame. 'This isn't justice, Pandora. Justice will be served by getting her and the bodyguard in court. Then the entire world will hear what happened to your daughter and the others.'

'No, she'll get off or a reduced sentence. People with money always do.'

Pandora's hand was on Grace's head as she smiled at me.

Then she let go of the lighter.

I SPENT two days in the hospital having my burns treated.

My instincts kicked in as soon as I saw Pandora drop the flame. I'd raised my arm to protect my face, but I would have gone up in flames with them if Jack hadn't pulled me back and out of that room. The smell of burning human flesh and Randolph's screams continued to live in my head even now.

'The doctors said you could go home tomorrow.'

Jack's voice was low, which I assumed was because Abbey was asleep in a chair behind him.

'It's about time.' My arm throbbed under the bandages. 'How long before your hair grows back?'

He was as bald as an egg, with a dark shadow covering the top of his skull, so it looked as if someone had turned him upside down and dipped him in chocolate.

Jack rubbed at his chrome dome. 'I don't know, but Tiffany likes it. She says I look like Bruce Willis.'

I laughed through the pain. 'More like Bruce Forsyth with that poor excuse of a moustache you're growing.'

He touched the gap between his nose and top lip.

'I need some hair up here to stay warm.'

The mention of heat brought back the last thing I remembered from that room.

'What's happening with Declan Blake?' The bodyguard Grace claimed had helped her with the abductions and murders.

Jack dragged his chair closer to me. 'For a hardened criminal, he's singing like a bird. First, he confirmed everything Randolph told us and admitted to threatening and bribing Green, Cole and Wallace to keep them quiet about what they knew of the missing teenagers. Then he led us to where most of the bodies were buried. And there's one more thing.' Darkness filled his expression.

'What's that?'

'He recorded many of his crimes on video.' Jack took a long breath. Like me, he'd become hardened to most things we'd seen, but some were still too terrible not to affect us. 'It was mainly teenage girls, but there were half a dozen boys as well.'

'Half a dozen!'

I stared beyond him at Abbey slumbering, hoping she was thinking about the football team or playing in her band.

'How many kids in total?'

'So far, we know of twenty.'

'Fuck! Fucking fuck fuck!'

I was glad for the pain in my arm because it stopped the anger consuming me.

'Has he confirmed what Grace told us?'

He nodded. 'He has. I also did a background check on her. Before she met and married Randolph, she'd spent time in several hospitals when she was younger for an extreme skin condition that was debilitating at the worst times. When I told Randolph this, he said he knew nothing about it. Blake claims that, after the first death, accident or not, Grace became obsessed with blood and fascinated with Countess Elizabeth Báthory. Have you heard of her?'

'I have. Countess Dracula.' I could see the lurid newspaper headlines now. 'What about Catherine Lilly?'

He shook his head. 'Nothing so far, but we're still looking. I'm sure there's more to come from Blake.'

I peered beyond him and at Abbey.

'And there were two bodies in the remains at the beauty parlour?'

'Forensics seems to think so.'

'Only seems? They don't know for definite?'

'Not yet. There were a lot of chemicals in the room that mixed in with the petrol Pandora had.'

'So she might have escaped?'

Jack shrugged. 'I don't think she wanted to.'

'I guess it's over then.'

He reached into his pocket, removed a bar of expensive dark chocolate and handed it to me.

'And that means we have two reasons to celebrate.'

I tore the wrapper off and put a large bit in my mouth, chewing it as I spoke.

'Why two reasons?'

'When you return to work, you'll be Detective Chief Inspector Flowers.'

The chocolate got stuck in my throat as I jerked up.

'Who told you?'

He grinned at me. 'You just did.'

I swallowed the chunk before it killed me. 'How did you know?'

'Who do you think mentioned it to Cane, Jen?'

Sitting in that bed wearing a hospital gown was the most vulnerable I'd felt in a long time.

'What about you, Jack? Don't you want to be a DCI?'

He rubbed at the stubble growing on his chin.

'Not now. I've got too much going on with Tiff to worry about that.'

'Marriage and a baby?'

He laughed. 'Possibly one, perhaps both.'

'Are you feeling better, Mum?'

Abbey was on her feet.

'I'm fine, love.' I stared at her and thought again about what I'd do if she went missing. Then I remembered the Wests. 'Is Francine okay?'

She narrowed her eyes as she approached me.

'Of course she is. We've been writing songs over the phone while you've been in here.'

'That's great, Abbey.'

I pulled at the bandage on my arm, trying to reach the itch underneath.

She sat on the bed. 'And I went to visit Grandma in the home. She's worried about you.'

This time I choked as my tongue crawled towards the back of my throat.

'What?'

'I said we'd see her when you get out of here. Is that okay?'

I took her hand. 'We'll do it tomorrow, love.'

Abbey was fine, the Wests were okay, and Jack was happy. And my promotion was on the horizon.

So I should have been fine.

But inside that clean, clinical hospital room, my head was full of smoke and fire.

THANK YOU!

Thank you, dear reader for purchasing this book.

If you enjoyed reading about Jen Flowers her story continues in these books:

The Detective Jen Flowers series
Book one: The Hashtag Killer.
Book two: Serial Killer.
Book three: Night Killer.
Book four: The Killer Inside Them

Many thanks to my wonderful wife for all her support and patience.

The Killer Inside Them edited by Alison Jack.

Extra special thanks to Karina Gallagher for being a dedicated reader of my work.

Cover design by James, GoOnWrite.com

ABOUT THE AUTHOR

Andrew French lives amongst faded seaside glamour on the North East coast of England. He likes gin and cats but not together, new music and old movies, curry and ice cream. Slow bike rides and long walks to the pub are his usual exercise, as well as flicking through the pages of good books and the memoirs of bad people.

Find out more at www.andrewsfrench.com

Facebook:

https://www.facebook.com/A-S-French-Author-150145625006018

Twitter:

www.twitter.com/andrewfrench100

Instagram:

www.instagram.com/andrewfrench100

And replies to all his email at mail@andrewsfrench.com

If you have the time, please leave a review at Amazon or Goodreads

Thank you!